TERROR IN THE STADIUM

Terror in the Stadium

LEFT BEHIND

>THE KIDS<

Jerry B. Jenkins

Tim LaHaye

WITH CHRIS FABRY

TYNDALE HOUSE PUBLISHERS, INC.
WHEATON, ILLINOIS

Visit Tyndale's exciting Web site at www.tyndale.com

Discover the latest Left Behind news at www.leftbehind.com

Published in association with the literary agency of Alive Communications, Inc., 7680 Goddard Street, Suite 200, Colorado Springs, CO 80920.

Edited by Curtis H. C. Lundgren

ISBN 0-8423-4299-0

Printed in the United States of America

08 07 06 05 04 03 02 01
 9   8   7   6   5   4   3   2   1

To Josh and Carl

Table of Contents

What's Gone On Before ix

1. At Death's Door 1
2. The Funeral 11
3. The Flight 23
4. The Secret Passage 37
5. The Visitor 49
6. Confession 61
7. The Surprise Meeting 75
8. Witnesses to History 89
9. Nicolae's Speech 103
10. Reason to Kill 115
11. The Consuming Fire 127
12. Death in the Stadium 139

About the Authors

What's Gone On Before

JUDD Thompson Jr. and the others in the Young Tribulation Force are in grave danger. A giant meteor has killed their close friend, John Preston.

Now, with new identities, the kids plan their next move. When the Global Community catches up to Judd's biker friend Pete, pilot Taylor Graham attempts a daring rescue. The kids are able to stop him before he needlessly kills a GC officer.

Lionel Washington and Mr. Stein retrieve some cash from Mr. Stein's office and return to the others. Mr. Stein is intent on going to the Meeting of the Witnesses in Israel, though he doesn't know how he will get there.

After a disagreement, Vicki Byrne and Judd separate. Vicki, Lionel, Conrad Graham, and Darrion Stahley rush back to Chicago to try to find Ryan's dog, Phoenix. They find him and Vicki's friend Charlie, being held by the

GC. After rescuing them, the kids search for a secret hideout.

Mr. Stein learns more about God as he and Judd read the Bible and study Tsion Ben-Judah's Web site. Judd answers E-mail questions from kids who beg to know God.

As they prepare for the Meeting of the Witnesses, another comet of judgment bears down on the earth. Judd is desperate to reach Vicki and the others with the news.

With bits of the comet Wormwood falling around them, Judd and Mr. Stein find the secret schoolhouse and warn their friends. Suddenly, the two surviving Morale Monitors, Melinda and Felicia, burst into the room. Melinda waves a gun and tells them to get on the ground.

Join the Young Tribulation Force as they battle the enemies of their souls.

ONE

At Death's Door

JUDD raised his hands and knelt with the others. Melinda pointed her gun around and tried to support Felicia, who was pale and almost unconscious, her head hanging.

"On your faces!" Melinda shouted.

Charlie, Vicki's weird friend, wandered in, holding a candle. His eyes grew large when he recognized the two Morale Monitors. "I didn't know the water was bad, I promise!"

"On the floor!" Melinda yelled.

What had Conrad and Lionel told Judd about the girls? He knew they were fiercely loyal to the Global Community and their leader, Commander Blancka. Vicki said she thought the GC had turned on them and wanted them dead. Judd watched for his chance to surprise them.

"You don't have to do this," Vicki said. "We're not going to hurt you."

"Shut up!" Melinda shouted. She stared at Vicki. "You guys all look weird. What happened to your hair?" Melinda let go of Felicia, and the girl fell to the floor. Mr. Stein was still kneeling with his hands folded in prayer.

Melinda fired into the ceiling, and plaster fell. "I said, on the ground!"

Nine of us, two of them, Judd thought. *If we rush Melinda, we can overpower her, but someone might get killed.*

Judd caught Lionel's eye. Lionel clenched his teeth and shook his head. Vicki crawled toward Felicia and put a hand on her neck.

"Touch her and you die!" Melinda said, pointing the gun at Vicki.

Judd lurched forward, but Melinda quickly put the gun in his face. "You want it first, Thompson?"

Mark grabbed Judd's ankles.

"Stop," Vicki said. "I feel a pulse." She put an ear over Felicia's face. "Hardly breathing. Help me get her to a bed."

Mr. Stein moved to help.

"Leave her alone!" Melinda shouted. She fired another bullet into the ceiling, sending the kids scrambling.

"She's dying," Vicki said. "There may not be much time."

At Death's Door

Melinda brushed dirty hair from her face. "Why would you help her?"

Vicki lifted Felicia's shoulders. "Put her in my room. It's closest."

Melinda didn't move.

"Judd, get hot water from the stove and some rags," Vicki said. "Conrad, drinking water. A lot of it."

"Not him," Melinda said, pointing to Conrad. She nodded to Shelly. "You."

"I'll get blankets, too," Shelly said.

Judd shoved a pot of water over the fire on the ancient stove. The schoolhouse still had no electricity.

"The rest of you stay here," he heard Melinda say from the other room. She called out, "And if you guys try to run, I'll shoot them."

Judd gathered rags and opened a drawer, where he found a heavy rolling pin. He banged it against his palm.

Vicki feared Felicia was near death. Mr. Stein helped prop up her head.

"If she drank from the well," he said, "there is nothing we can do. The Scriptures say thousands will die from Wormwood."

Melinda barked orders in the other room.

3

Shelly brought water and blankets. Vicki
tried to get Felicia to drink, but she didn't
respond. "If we can get her to drink, it might
wash out some of the poison."

Judd brought the warm water and rags to
Vicki's room, and Vicki cleaned Felicia's face.
She grabbed the rolling pin from him. "You
want to get us killed, Judd?"

"We have to do something," he said.

Vicki tossed it under the bed. Melinda
came running.

"If we can't get Felicia to drink clean
water," Vicki said, "well . . . it doesn't look
good."

Melinda ordered the others into the next
room. Judd glanced at Vicki on his way out.

"Why are you doing this?" Melinda asked
Vicki.

"She's sick. Why are *you* doing this?"

Melinda laughed. "I'm taking every one
of you back. You're enemies of the Global
Community."

"So are you," Vicki said.

"What? I've been loyal to the GC since the
day I signed on as a Morale Monitor."

"Then you don't know?" Vicki said.

"Know what?"

"The GC is after you. I'm surprised they
haven't killed you already."

Melinda stared. "You're lying. Why would they be after us?"

Felicia coughed and gagged, turning in the bed. She grabbed her stomach and screamed, "Make it stop! Make it stop!"

Vicki tried to hold her down, but Felicia clawed at Vicki's face. "Help me!" Vicki yelled.

"Felicia, it's me," Melinda said as she helped Vicki. "Try to drink some good water."

"I don't want a drink!" Felicia screamed. She writhed and fell back, unconscious again.

Vicki felt for a pulse. Felicia's heart was racing.

"I have to get her to a hospital," Melinda said.

"Impossible," Vicki said. "She'll be dead before you get to the main road. And if the GC finds you, you'll be dead too."

Melinda stared out the window.

"Did you drink from the well?" Vicki said.

Melinda shook her head. "I had the cup to my mouth when she fell and started shaking."

"Wormwood," Vicki muttered.

"Worm what?"

"The comet's name," Vicki said. "The Bible

predicted it would fall and poison the water. It also said people would die."

Melinda rolled her eyes. "That's right, you're part of the cult."

Vicki ignored her. "It happened, didn't it?"

Melinda stared at Felicia.

"Did she drink a lot?" Vicki said.

Melinda nodded.

Vicki handed Melinda a drink of fresh water. "You have to be thirsty."

Melinda eyed it warily. "How do I know it's not poisoned?"

Vicki grabbed it, took a drink, and handed it back.

Melinda sipped the water, then drank deeply. Vicki said, "How did you find us?"

"You came back for the dog. The GC planted a chip in his neck that sends out a signal. Felicia and I grabbed the locator and followed."

"You were in GC headquarters?" Vicki said.

"We wanted to find you guys bad."

"What took so long then?"

"We lost the signal, but we spotted Lionel at a pay phone. We tried to follow him, but he was too fast. Took us a couple of days to find this place."

"The GC didn't see you?" Vicki said.

Melinda squinted. "How did you know the GC are after us?"

"Commander Blancka's been killed by the GC," Vicki said. "People who had anything to do with the Morale Monitors are being wiped out."

Vicki dripped water into Felicia's mouth. "My guess is that the GC wanted to erase any evidence that we ever existed. Didn't want to look bad."

Melinda looked away. "They did come after us. We saw them whack Blancka and figured we'd be next. I thought if we could catch Stein or any of you, we'd prove our loyalty."

"And save your own skin."

"Exactly," Melinda said. She stuck her head in the next room and pointed to Shelly. "I saw rope outside. Bring it in here. And don't get any ideas about running if you care about your friends."

Felicia spat water. Her eyes were red and hideous. Her skin, pale when she had arrived, now looked green.

What a terrible way to die, Vicki thought.

"I can't breathe," Felicia gasped.

"Drink more water," Vicki pleaded. "It's the only thing—"

Felicia grabbed Vicki's arm. "I can feel it going through me," she wheezed. "It's like acid, eating me up."

Vicki screamed for Judd. Melinda let him through.

"You know CPR, right?" Vicki said.

Judd felt Felicia's wrist.

"She has a pulse," Vicki said. "It's her breathing."

"Do something!" Melinda said.

Judd put his mouth over Felicia's and blew hard. The girl's cheeks puffed out.

"No good," Judd said. "Airway's blocked. Or maybe her throat's tightened up."

"What can we do?" Vicki said.

"I'm not sure," Judd said. He pulled out his pocketknife. "Hand me that ballpoint pen."

Judd took the pen apart, then leaned over Felicia, his hands shaking.

Mr. Stein pushed past Melinda, knelt, and tilted Felicia's head. "Put the pen in the boiling water, Judd; then sterilize the knife over the fire. Hurry!"

Melinda looked over Mr. Stein's shoulder. "Is she going to be okay?"

"It may only prolong her agony," Mr. Stein said, "but we have to try." He shouted for Judd to return. "There's no time. She's turning blue!"

Judd rushed back with the pen and knife. Mr. Stein made a small cut at the base of Felicia's throat. Vicki wiped away the blood as Mr. Stein inserted the pen.

"You're going to kill her!" Melinda screamed.

As Mr. Stein blew through the pen, Judd said, "She'll die if we don't get her some air."

Vicki put a hand on Melinda's shoulder. She jerked away, scowling, then went to check on the others. Color returned to Felicia's face as Vicki watched her lungs fill.

Vicki knelt by her ear. "Felicia, I don't know if you can hear me, but I have to tell you something. God loves you. He died for you so you could live with him. If you can hear me, pray this with me—"

"Get away!" Melinda shouted as she ran back in, pushing Mr. Stein away as well.

Felicia opened her eyes and stared at Melinda. The pen-tube in her neck looked eerie. She tried to take a breath, but her lungs didn't fill. Then came a horrible gurgling sound.

Mr. Stein felt the girl's wrist. He stood and left the room. Judd followed.

"What?" Melinda said. "What happened?"

Vicki looked away and covered her mouth. Mr. Stein returned with a sheet. He pulled the pen from Felicia's neck and draped the sheet over her body.

Vicki couldn't hold back the tears.

"You can't," Lionel said, grabbing Judd's arm. "The gun might go off and kill somebody."

"I've had about fifteen chances to knock her down," Judd said. "I know I can do it."

"But you can't be sure."

"Then let's both get her."

Lionel shook his head. "You heard Vicki talking to her. She's getting through. Don't blow it now by going all macho."

"And if she comes in here and blows you and Conrad away, you'll wish I had."

Vicki wiped her eyes.

"What did you say to her?" Melinda said.

"I wanted her to know God loves her."

Melinda's eyes glazed. "You still think there's a God after all that's happened?"

"After all that's happened, I can't believe you don't."

Melinda pulled Vicki to her feet. "Get in there with the rest of them."

From the corner of her eye, Vicki saw Judd fly through the doorway. "No!" she screamed, as the gun went off.

TWO

The Funeral

LIONEL found Judd and Melinda struggling on the floor. The gun had been knocked to the far wall. Vicki lay motionless atop Felicia's body. Lionel held Melinda while Judd grabbed the gun. Melinda kicked free and retreated to the corner, panting.

"Vick!" Judd screamed, rushing to her. "Are you hit?"

Lionel and Judd gently rolled Vicki onto her back. Her mouth was bloody. Judd patted her cheek until she came to.

Vicki felt her lip and winced. "I heard the gun. What happened?"

"We've got Melinda under control," Judd said. "She's not going to hurt anybody."

Vicki gasped. "You rushed her!"

"I had to do something," Judd said.

"Things *were* under control. Melinda

11

wasn't going to shoot anybody. You could have gotten me killed!"

Lionel waved Conrad into the room, then looked at Judd and Vicki. "We have to talk."

Conrad kept an eye on Melinda while Judd, Vicki, and Lionel met upstairs.

"We've got decisions to make," Lionel said, "and having you two at each other's throats is not gonna help. You guys promised to work together, but that's not happening."

"We can work together," Judd said.

Vicki held a rag to her bloody lip and rolled her eyes.

"First, what do we do with Melinda?" Lionel said.

"And with people like Charlie?" Judd said.

"He's not a threat," Vicki said. "He just doesn't understand things yet."

"He didn't listen," Judd said. "He drank a little water when we told him not to, and he's the one Melinda and Felicia—"

"Melinda said she followed Lionel," Vicki said. "Besides, he's not going to run off and bring the GC back with him. He seems really interested in God. Give him a couple weeks."

"Melinda's another story," Judd said.

"What are you going to do, shoot her?" Vicki said.

"We ought to hold her. Lock her up."

"That's cruel," Vicki said. "This isn't a

prison. Besides, she's hurting. She just lost her best friend."

"She threatened to shoot us! And she wanted to take us all back to the GC. What do you want to do, let her go?"

Vicki took the rag away. Her lip had stopped bleeding but was still swollen. "We have to get her to trust us."

"Trust *us*?" Judd said.

Lionel looked closer at Vicki's lip. "Wish we had ice."

"We will once we get the generator started," Vicki said. She looked out the window. "It's a risk keeping Melinda or letting her go. I think we have to let her make the choice."

Judd shook his head. "That makes no sense. She's made her choice. She's GC."

"You don't know what she told me," Vicki said. "She knows the Global Community is after her."

"And she suddenly comes over to our side, just like that?"

"Not right away," Vicki said, "but a little compassion, a little friendship and concern could go a long way. Outside, she's dead."

Judd put his elbows on his knees and sighed. "We need to bury Felicia."

"After the funeral, I say we put it to Melinda," Vicki said.

"And if she decides to go back to the GC?" Judd said.

"Then we'll have to find a new place," Vicki said.

"And that wrecks Z's idea of using this place for storage."

Vicki paused. "Let me talk to her."

Vicki asked Conrad to join her in the hall. She took the gun and emptied the bullets into her pocket. "Does she have any more ammo on her?"

Conrad handed her a handful of bullets. "This is all both of them were carrying."

"I need to speak with Melinda alone," Vicki said. "Did she say anything to you?"

Conrad shook his head. "She just stared out the window."

Vicki called for Phoenix, and together they went back into the room to see Melinda.

Melinda closed her eyes.

"You have three options," Vicki said. "Take your chances with the GC. Run as far from them as you can. Or stay with us."

"I'd rather die," Melinda said.

Vicki nodded. "And you probably will. They killed Commander Blancka."

"When I tell them you guys are here—"

"You won't have a chance," Vicki said. She

14

drew close to Melinda and knelt. "They'll shoot you on sight."

"Then I'll hide."

"Sooner or later they'll catch you," Vicki said.

Phoenix ambled over to Melinda and swished his tail back and forth. Soon he put his head on Melinda's lap. She didn't even seem to notice.

Vicki turned the gun over in her hands. "If you stayed, we'd offer you protection and food. They wouldn't find you."

"In return for . . ."

"Everybody pitches in," Vicki said. "Plus, you'd attend our studies."

"I'm not going to believe like you guys," Melinda said. "Ever."

"Maybe not," Vicki said. "But you have to admit, it's a better deal than Commander Blancka got."

Phoenix nuzzled Melinda's hand. The girl drew back. Phoenix licked the girl's arm, and she put her hand back on Phoenix's head.

Vicki handed the gun to Melinda and stood. "This is yours." She paused in the doorway. "The guys will dig Felicia's grave at sunup. We'll have the funeral in the afternoon. We'd like you to be there."

Melinda took the gun. "What if I take off tonight?"

That would change everything. Their lives would be thrown into turmoil. Vicki's plans for the old schoolhouse would be wrecked.

"Your choice," Vicki said. "If you have to, you have to."

Vicki closed the door, then opened it a crack. "If you go, take blankets with you. It's going to be nippy tonight."

Vicki put food and blankets by Melinda's door and went to bed, listening for any sign of Melinda leaving. At midnight she opened her door and saw the food still in the hallway, but the blankets were gone.

"Please, God," Vicki said, "convince her to stay."

Vicki wrestled with leaving. Could God have brought them here only to have them abandon the place? Was the dream of training kids just that—a dream?

The next morning Vicki found Judd and Mr. Stein in the kitchen.

"I see our guest is still here," Judd said.

"How do you know?" Vicki said.

"Looked in her window," Judd said. He returned Vicki's icy stare. "We have a right to know if she's gone or not, don't we?"

"Don't blow this for me, Judd."

Mr. Stein said, "That girl has been through

so much. I only hope we can get through to her before something happens to her."

Mr. Stein used Judd's laptop to log on to Tsion Ben-Judah's Web site. Judd and Vicki ate in silence.

"The rabbi writes about the Meeting of the Witnesses," Mr. Stein said.

"Still scheduled for next week?" Vicki said.

"Yes. And thousands of house churches have begun—run by Jews who have become believers in Jesus as Messiah."

"House churches," Vicki said. "I like that. This is going to be a house church for the Young Tribulation Force."

"It's going to be more than that," Judd said. "Z is going to run supplies through here and help feed people who won't obey Carpathia."

"What else does it say?" Vicki said.

"The house churches base their teachings on Tsion Ben-Judah's daily messages over the Internet," Mr. Stein said. "Though the Global Community urges everyone to join the Enigma Babylon One World Faith, tens of thousands of such churches meet every day.

"Tsion urges congregations to send their leaders to the great meeting, in spite of warnings from the GC. Nicolae Carpathia has tried again and again to cancel it."

Mr. Stein scrolled through the message excitedly. "Oh, listen to this! Dr. Ben-Judah writes, 'We will be in Jerusalem as scheduled, with or without your approval, permission, or promised protection. The glory of the Lord will be our rear guard.'"

"He called Carpathia's bluff," Judd said.

"We must get the generator started," Mr. Stein said. "I want to be able to keep your computer going twenty-four hours a day while the meetings are taking place."

Conrad burst into the kitchen, out of breath. "Judd, come with me."

Judd followed Conrad around to the front and down the hill. Shelly stood holding a dirty shovel beside a deep hole. Mark pecked at a rock in the bottom. Conrad pointed. "We were digging the grave and we hit that. Then we found another rock the same size, and another, and now there's a whole section of them, along with big beams of wood."

"Looks like a tomb," Judd said. "Have you seen what's inside?"

"It's like they're cemented together," Mark said.

"Cover it over and we'll dig the grave farther up the hill," Judd said.

"What?" Mark said. "We're almost—"

"Melinda is still inside," Judd said.

"What's that got to do with—"

"This may turn out to be nothing," Judd interrupted. "Then again, it might be something we don't want her to see. We'll dig again after the funeral."

Vicki was glad when Melinda joined them at the kitchen table later that morning. Melinda eyed Mr. Stein and pushed back a plate of food. "If you guys hadn't gotten away, the commander would still be alive. Felicia too."

"They were going to execute me," Mr. Stein said. "We had to do something."

Lionel made a wooden stretcher and placed Felicia's body on it. Melinda walked beside Vicki as they followed the procession up the hill to the burial site.

Conrad and Judd gently placed the wrapped body in the hole. Vicki put a hand on Melinda's shoulder as the group awkwardly looked at one another.

Finally, Lionel spoke. "I didn't know Felicia well, but I do know how dedicated she was as a Morale Monitor. She would have made a great member of the Young Trib Force."

Mr. Stein shifted from one foot to another. "I lost my only daughter in the earthquake." He turned to Melinda. "I am deeply saddened for your loss."

"It should've been me," Melinda said. "If I'd have taken the first drink, you'd be burying me."

"You're here for a reason," Vicki said.

Melinda backed away. "I know why you're being so nice. You want me to keep quiet about this place. But that would betray what Felicia and I were trying to do in the first place."

Judd's cell phone rang.

"I won't stay here," Melinda continued. "And you can't stop me."

Judd handed the phone to Mr. Stein as Melinda raced toward the schoolhouse. "Taylor Graham," Judd said. "He got the number from Boyd at the gas station. Said it was urgent."

As Conrad and Lionel shoveled dirt into the grave, Judd approached Vicki. "Sorry about Melinda. Guess we're going to have to move."

"I thought I was getting through to her," Vicki said.

"Maybe you were," Judd said. "People have to make their own choices."

Mr. Stein snapped the phone shut, his face

ashen. "It is a miracle," he said. "A true miracle of God. I am going to Israel. I am going to the Meeting of the Witnesses."

THREE

The Flight

JUDD couldn't believe it. Mr. Stein going to Israel?

"Taylor has access to a plane," Mr. Stein said. "He said there is an airfield near us."

"You know where he got that plane," Judd said. "It's GC property."

"I thought Taylor didn't want anything to do with us," Vicki said.

"He knows I have money," Mr. Stein said. "He said he wants to keep his promise. I think he needs cash."

"Wait," Judd said. "If he's going after Carpathia, why is he going to Israel? Nick's not there."

Mr. Stein shrugged. "Perhaps he will continue to New Babylon."

Judd sighed. "Something's not right. It may be a GC trap."

"You know Taylor would never let the GC

take him alive," Vicki said. "I'm happy for Mr. Stein."

"Does sound weird," Lionel said. "And the GC will be looking for that plane."

"I'm leaving that to Taylor," Mr. Stein said. "I need to contact a guide to help me in Israel. I've never been there."

Judd's mind swirled. "I've been twice. I could help you."

"I had dibs on the next trip," Lionel said. "Besides, we're needed here. If we have to move everybody to—"

"We're not moving," Vicki said. "Even if Melinda leaves, this is where we're supposed to be."

"Vick—," Judd said.

"Trust me on this," Vicki interrupted. "God gave us this school for a reason. We're not running."

"Vick, Melinda could lead them right to you," Judd said.

"We stand or fall here," Vicki said. "Take Lionel and go—if it's okay with you, Mr. Stein."

"Yes, I would love the company," Mr. Stein said.

"Then it's settled," Vicki said.

Vicki found Melinda gathering supplies at the schoolhouse.

"Before you go, I want you to have something," Vicki said. She handed some bullets and Felicia's gun to her.

"Why are you giving me these?" Melinda said.

"In case you meet up with the GC. I don't think you'll use them against us."

Melinda rolled the bullets in her hand and sat. "How'd you guys change your looks? I almost didn't recognize you."

Vicki explained, without telling about Z. "We have new IDs and everything. Hopefully it'll protect us from the GC."

Melinda sighed heavily. "The Global Community promised a better life. Conrad and Lionel don't know."

"Know what?"

"Where I came from. What I've seen."

"Tell me," Vicki said. She sat and stared at Melinda.

Finally, the girl spoke. "I grew up in the East. My dad sold insurance and we moved around a lot. Pittsburgh. Buffalo. Richmond. It was almost like being in the military. You make some friends, and it's time to move again."

"That's tough," Vicki said.

"Yeah, but not as tough as it got after the disappearances. That whole thing tanked my dad's business. Things got rough at home. He drank a lot and screamed at me. I'd take off for a few days, then come back."

"What about your mom?"

Melinda shook her head.

"How'd you meet Felicia?" Vicki said.

"School. Her family life wasn't any better. We'd sit at lunch and plan our escape. She had an uncle who invited us. Even mailed us some money. One Monday morning we got on a bus and headed north. Thought our problems were solved." Melinda closed her eyes. "That was the worst week of my life, until now."

"What happened?" Vicki said.

"I can't tell you everything," Melinda said. "It's too awful. The guy was a creep. He sold drugs. He basically locked us up."

"That's terrible," Vicki said.

"Only thing we could do was watch TV. That's when we saw Nicolae Carpathia. Everything he did—peace treaties, an end to war—that's what we were looking for. Sounded like heaven on earth. Felicia and I decided to get out of there and sign up."

"You escaped?" Vicki said.

"We tricked a guy into letting us out. Told him we'd show him where Felicia's uncle hid his stash."

"Cool," Vicki said.

"We found a GC post and heard about the

Morale Monitors. Felicia and I signed up, and they sent us into training."

"That's where you met Conrad and Lionel," Vicki said.

Melinda nodded. "Our first job was Chicago."

"You thought the Morale Monitors would be the answer."

Melinda slumped in her chair. "I don't know what went wrong. I blamed it on Lionel and Conrad at first. I couldn't believe they'd work against us. Then Commander Blancka . . . it doesn't make sense."

Vicki didn't want to come on too strong, but she knew Melinda needed to hear the truth. "Can I give you my theory?" she said.

Melinda rubbed her forehead. "I think I know what's coming, but go ahead."

"I met this journalist," Vicki said, "a guy who's a lot smarter than me, and he investigated Carpathia and the whole Global Community plan. Melinda, their goal is not world peace. Carpathia and his people want control."

"I don't mind people being in control if they want peace for everybody."

"They don't," Vicki said. "They want to run the world, and if anyone gets in their way or messes up . . . well, look at what happened to Commander Blancka."

"Pretty hard to believe," Melinda said.

"Everything I'm telling you was predicted in the Bible. The disappearances, the earthquake, the peace treaty with Israel, the comets—everything. I can show you."

"Religion's not my thing," Melinda said.

"Mine either," Vicki said, "but this is not religion. This is the truth. Stay. I'll explain it all. What do you have to lose?"

"You really think the GC will do the same to me as they did to the commander?"

"If I were you, I wouldn't want to chance it," Vicki said.

Melinda rolled the gun over and looked at Vicki. "All right. But the minute I find out you're hiding something or lying to me, I'm out of here."

"Deal," Vicki said.

Judd talked with Taylor Graham by phone and explained that he and Lionel would accompany Mr. Stein.

"I only agreed to take one," Taylor said.

Judd handed the phone to Mr. Stein.

"How many seats are there on that plane?" Stein said. "Six? Good, then we will have three extras for anyone else that might—"

Mr. Stein held the phone away from his ear. Taylor Graham yelled something.

"It's my money," Mr. Stein said. "If they don't come, I stay."

After a few moments, Mr. Stein handed the phone back to Judd.

"All right, listen," Taylor Graham said. "There's a landing strip in a ritzy development about ten miles from you."

"The earthquake didn't destroy—?"

"These people have more money than Carpathia himself," Taylor said. "The strip's been repaired. The problem is tight security. There's a guard 24-7 and a fence all the way around. I need you to turn on the landing lights. I'll wait two minutes at the end of the runway. If you're not there, I'm gone."

"Why don't we just come to you?" Judd said.

Taylor laughed. "It'd take too much time."

"Isn't there anywhere else you could land?" Judd said.

"I've scoped it out," Taylor said. "This is the way it goes down. If you can't make this happen, forget it."

"We'll be there," Judd said.

Taylor gave Judd the exact location and the time he would arrive.

"We'll need to leave soon if we're going to make it," Judd said when he hung up.

Suddenly there was an explosion, and a

grinding sound came from the other end of the house. Judd and Mr. Stein rushed through billowy black smoke and found Lionel high-fiving Conrad.

Conrad stood by the generator, covered with grease. "We did it!"

Judd inspected the machine. "As long as you can find gas, this should give you power."

"We found three underground gas tanks," Conrad said. "Must be Z's work."

"Get cleaned up," Judd said to Lionel. "We're heading out." Judd took Vicki aside. "Is Melinda gone?"

"She's staying for now."

"Good," Judd said. "I'll leave my laptop so you guys can watch the coverage of the meetings. Don't let her know about Taylor or where we're going."

Vicki nodded. "I know. Give us an update when you can."

"You can take two of the cycles and ditch them," Conrad said. "They're just sitting here."

Judd sensed something was wrong with Conrad. "Did you want to go with us?"

Conrad shook his head. "It's my brother. Talk some sense into Taylor if you can. He's going to get himself killed."

Judd patted Conrad on the shoulder as Darrion slipped an envelope into Judd's hand. "Give Taylor this. Maybe it will help."

Mr. Stein showed Vicki where he had hidden the rest of his money. "Use as much of it as you need."

Judd and Lionel pushed the cycles to the road and started them. Traveling after dark was difficult. Judd wasn't familiar with the roads. Finally, he spotted the well-lit water tower Taylor had described.

"It's only a couple of miles from here," Judd said to Mr. Stein sitting behind him.

When they came within a few hundred yards of the gated community, Judd and Lionel turned off their cycles and hid them in some tall grass. They walked the rest of the way.

Mr. Stein huffed and puffed as he carried the heavy duffel bag filled with cash. "How much longer?"

"We've got about an hour to figure out how to get inside," Judd said.

"Are there security guards all around?" Lionel said.

"Only one," Judd said, "but I'm sure they have cameras and sensors around the fence. We have to time this just right."

Mr. Stein wiped his brow. "I don't know if I can handle this much excitement."

Judd spotted a delivery truck. "Wait here."

Judd ran through a field and darted to the

other side of the road as the delivery truck stopped by the guardhouse. Judd saw a camera above him and stayed in the shadows.

"Okay, we got one package for Kendall, number 418, and another one for Miller," the man in the truck said.

"Miller again?" the guard said. "Busy place."

The guard signed for the packages and the driver left. Judd checked his watch. Only forty-five minutes before Taylor touched down.

"What did you see?" Lionel asked when Judd returned.

"It's tight. They don't even let delivery guys inside. But I have an idea."

Judd took some cash and told Mr. Stein and Lionel to stay on the south side of the fence. "When you hear Taylor's plane, climb over and meet me at the end of the airstrip."

Judd grabbed a motorcycle and raced to a nearby gas station. "Anybody know where I can get a pizza around here?"

A girl behind the counter gave him a name and phone number. "It won't do you any good," she said. "They don't deliver to a pay phone."

"If you order, would they deliver?" Judd said.

"They might," she said coyly.

Judd pulled out a fifty-dollar bill. "Would this convince you?"

The girl looked over her glasses and snatched the bill. "You must want a pizza pretty bad."

A noisy car chugged into the station thirty-five minutes later. Judd handed the man a fifty, and he stared at it. "I can't make change for this."

"Keep it," Judd said.

"You mean it?" the man said.

Judd jumped on his motorcycle and roared off, holding the pizza tightly. Taylor was only ten minutes from touchdown.

Judd pulled into the guard station and smiled. "Got a delivery here."

The guard eyed Judd warily. "Where's your sign?"

"They're trying to save money," Judd said as he looked around the guard's station and whistled. "I've never delivered here before. Is this the place where the planes land?"

"Yeah. Who's the pizza for?"

"You control the runway lights in here?"

The guard leaned close. "Who's the pizza for?"

"Sorry," Judd said. "It's for Miller. Which house is it?"

The guard looked at his logbook.

"Is there a problem?" Judd said.

The guard picked up a phone. "They're supposed to tell security when they order . . . Yes, Mrs. Miller, this is the front gate."

Judd saw a panel of switches for the runway lights on the office wall. He put the pizza down and climbed onto his motorcycle.

"Ma'am, we have a pizza here. Did you order—"

Judd sped under the barrier and past the well-manicured shrubbery.

"Hey, come back here!" the guard yelled.

Judd rounded the corner and shot through a yard. He hid the bike behind a tree and sprinted into the shadows. Moments later a jeep roared by. Judd ran to the guardhouse. A jet passed overhead.

An alarm rang, and Judd saw Lionel and Mr. Stein on a small monitor. They crawled over the fence near the runway.

"Right on time," Judd muttered. He flipped switches and bolted outside. Judd ran behind houses. Dogs barked. When the plane touched down, he raced toward it. Lionel and Mr. Stein stayed low at the end of the runway. Taylor rolled to a stop and opened the door. Mr. Stein and Lionel scampered aboard and waved for Judd. The engines screamed as Judd jumped into the plane.

"Everybody buckle in!" Taylor shouted.
"We've got company."

Through the cockpit window Judd saw the
jeep coming at them. Taylor swerved left,
then right and off the runway to miss the
oncoming car. When the jeep passed, Taylor
gunned the engine. Within a few seconds
they were airborne and heading toward the
Middle East.

FOUR

The Secret Passage

Judd couldn't sleep. When the plane left Chicago, Mr. Stein sighed with relief. His eyes shimmered with excitement.

Judd asked Mr. Stein where they would stay in Jerusalem, but he wouldn't discuss it.

"I can make us a reservation," Judd said.

Mr. Stein held up a hand. "God will provide."

Taylor tuned in a Global Community frequency and listened. He had a stolen GC codebook and followed the security forces' movements.

"Did you kill anyone getting this plane?" Judd said.

"Why are you so worried about the GC?" Taylor said. "They're your enemy."

"There's a chance anybody can turn around," Judd said. "A lot of GC people were forced into service. Our job is just to give the message."

"Well, my job is to stop the GC wherever I can and, ultimately, to kill Nicolae Carpathia."

"I wouldn't advertise that if I were you," Lionel said.

"Before I get to him," Taylor continued, "I'll probably have to take out other GC posts."

Judd shook his head.

"I know you all want to tell people about Jesus and do good stuff so God will like you and all that. I've told you before, if that rings your bell, go ahead. But I've seen what the GC does to good people. They're destroying everything I know and love. They talk peace, but they're armed to the teeth. They talk freedom, but they send people to prison. Oh, sorry. They call them reeducation camps."

"You can't do it alone," Judd said.

"Maybe not," Taylor said. "But I'm giving them a run for their money." Taylor eyed Mr. Stein. "Speaking of which, where's the cash you promised?"

Mr. Stein opened a satchel and produced an envelope filled with large bills. Taylor grinned. "This should keep me going for a while."

Judd remembered the letter in his pocket.

He handed it to Taylor. "Darrion asked me to give you this."

Taylor took it and said, "How's Conrad?"

"He's worried about you," Lionel said.

The radio squawked, and a man gave a report about a plane using a private airfield in Illinois. "A local guard on the ground reports seeing a GC insignia on the side of the plane," the man said. "This may be the stolen jet we're looking for."

"We're way ahead of them," Taylor said, opening the letter and checking his watch. "We should be in Tel Aviv in good time."

"Why Tel Aviv?" Judd said.

"This plane needs a new paint job. I've lined up somebody to do it." Taylor read Darrion's note privately.

Lionel signaled for Judd. "Do you realize the danger we're in? This is a stolen airplane, the pilot's killed several GC personnel, crashed a GC helicopter, and he isn't finished yet."

"I've been thinking the same thing," Judd said.

Taylor stuffed the letter in his shirt and waved Judd forward. "All right, you guys are taking a chance riding with me. You deserve to know what's happened.

"Some people did get killed at the base,

but the GC press reported that it was a terrorist attack. It was just me. I wired explosives in the other planes and choppers. They were supposed to explode just after I took off. A couple of guys saw me and scrambled before I could get away. Those were the only two who got killed, I swear.

"I'm not a killing machine, and I don't want innocent people to get hurt. But this is a war. I'm going to stop the Global Community, or at least slow them down as much as I can."

"You could do a lot more damage to them on our side," Judd said.

"You guys are weak," Taylor said. "These people don't understand anything but strength. Plus, you don't have a plan."

"Our goal is to change people one at a time," Lionel said. "From reading the Bible, we know we can't overthrow the system, but having people on the inside will help."

"You do it your way. I'll do it mine."

"Why did you let us come with you?" Judd said.

"I need the money. Now I have it. This will be my last run with you guys."

"What about the return flight?" Mr. Stein said.

"Never discussed that," Taylor said.

"What?!" Judd yelled.

"Calm down. It's nothing personal. I've got a job to do and I can't wait in Israel."

"I'm through talking to him," Judd said. He stomped back to his seat and strapped himself in.

Lionel leaned close to Taylor and said something. The two talked for a few minutes, then Taylor motioned for them all to sit. "Some turbulence up ahead. Buckle in and get some rest."

Vicki kept track of Melinda and tried to make her as comfortable as possible. When Melinda asked about Judd, Vicki hesitated. "I'm not going to lie to you, but I don't feel I can tell you the truth."

"You don't trust me," Melinda said.

Vicki smiled. "You threatened us. Give it some time."

Melinda nodded. "Okay. But if you lie to me and I find out, I'm gone."

Conrad came through the door, out of breath and covered with dirt. He glanced at Melinda, then turned to Vicki. "Can I see you a minute? Alone?"

Vicki excused herself and went outside with Conrad. He led her toward the river to the original site of Felicia's grave.

"I got up early to figure this out," Conrad said. He told Vicki about the stone he had found and Judd's instructions to dig it up after the burial. "With all the excitement about the trip, we didn't have time."

Vicki climbed into the freshly dug hole. On one side, she saw stones intricately woven together. Conrad had chipped away at the underground wall until one of the stones came loose. Vicki helped work the stone back and forth until it was almost out. Conrad used the end of his shovel, and the stone dropped inside. It fell a few feet with a *thunk*.

"It's hollow in there," Conrad said. He stuck his head through the opening and peered inside.

"Don't do that," Vicki said. "You don't know what's in there."

"Maybe it's some kind of vault," Conrad said.

"Why would they put it out here?" Vicki said.

"I'll try to get another stone out," Conrad said. "Get a flashlight."

When Vicki returned, Conrad had opened a hole big enough to crawl through. Vicki shone the light into the darkness. There were cobwebs and some debris on the dirt floor, but the room looked clear.

Conrad crawled through and dropped to

the ground. His voice echoed. "It's at least six feet tall. Come on down."

Vicki looked at the house. No one stirred. Conrad helped her down.

"This is no vault," Conrad said. "The thing keeps on going in both directions."

Vicki followed as they walked away from the house. The walls of the passage looked ancient, but they were in good shape.

"Whoever built this sure knew what they were doing," Conrad said.

"What if it caves in?" Vicki said.

Conrad banged the top of the passage with his hand and winced. "It's solid."

The passage dipped downhill as they walked farther. The earthen floor became muddy.

"Stop!" Vicki said. She put a finger to her lips. "Hear that? It's water."

Conrad kept going. Finally, they came to the end. The flashlight shone on a thick, wooden door with a huge padlock. The lock was rusty. Conrad banged it with the flashlight but it didn't open.

"What do you think's on the other side?" Conrad said.

"We'll have to go outside to find out," Vicki said.

The two traced their way back to the hole.

Conrad picked up an old piece of cloth from the ground and stuffed it in his pocket. Vicki started to climb out, but Conrad tugged at her sleeve. "Let's see where it goes the other way."

The passage led uphill. At times it was so steep Vicki and Conrad had to crawl. They found another door in better shape. However, instead of a padlock, there was only a round door knocker.

"I've seen these in those old horror movies," Vicki said.

"Yeah, the castles with all the fog."

Conrad pulled on the knocker, but the door didn't budge. The sound echoed throughout the passage. He knocked a few more times.

"Guess there's nobody home," Conrad said. "Let's get outta here."

They climbed out of the hole and brushed themselves off. Conrad pointed toward the river. "I'm going to see where it ends."

Someone ran from the house. Shelly rounded the corner and spotted Vicki and Conrad. "Come quick!" she shouted. "The house is haunted."

"What's going on?" Vicki said.

"It's weird," Shelly said. "We heard something banging. When we went downstairs, it stopped."

Approaching Tel Aviv, Judd woke Lionel. "What did you and Taylor talk about?" Judd said.

Lionel rubbed his eyes and kept his voice low. "Darrion told me what she wrote in the letter. I figured it had to affect him."

"Did it?"

"He didn't break down crying, but I could tell she hit a nerve," Lionel said. "He said he'd do anything he could to help her."

"What did she say in the letter?"

"She thanked him for everything he did for her family. Talked about what happened to her dad just before he died. Then she said if her dad and mom were alive they'd want him to believe in God too."

"Pretty powerful," Judd said.

Lionel patted Judd on the shoulder. "Keep praying."

As the plane touched down on the outskirts of Tel Aviv, that was exactly what Judd was doing.

Vicki and Conrad followed Shelly back to the schoolhouse. Charlie, who had survived swallowing some of the bitter water, was spooked.

"I heard the noise. It's a ghost, I know it," Charlie said. "It must be a big one, and it must really be mad at somebody 'cause it kept banging."

"It's not a ghost," Vicki said, putting a hand on Charlie's arm. "Come on."

They filed down the narrow staircase to the musty room under the kitchen. One bare bulb lit the area.

Melinda followed. Conrad grabbed Vicki's arm. "What about her?"

"She'll find out sooner or later," Vicki whispered. "Maybe she'll trust us if we let her see."

"It came from over there," Shelly said, pointing to a stack of wooden pallets.

The kids moved the pallets to the other side of the room. Spiders and bugs scampered away. Conrad inspected the wall but found no door. He tapped, but the wood was solid.

"Look at that," Vicki said.

On the floor, barely visible under all the dirt and dust, was an old rug, about four feet square.

"This is interesting," Conrad said.

He jerked it away, and everyone coughed. When the dust cleared, Vicki knelt and inspected the floor. As she looked closely, Vicki saw the outline of a trapdoor. Conrad pulled out a pocketknife, but the wood was too heavy to pry open. Mark brought a crowbar and managed to lift it.

Vicki turned on the flashlight and peered into the darkness. Another set of rickety stairs led to an area about the size of a large bedroom. Vicki climbed down. There were no windows. They were well below ground level.

In the corner was a table with an oil lamp. A dusty book lay beside it. Vicki brushed it off, and flakes of leather crumbled in her hands. It crackled when she opened it.

"It's a Bible!" Vicki said. The pages were so brittle she closed it for fear of tearing them.

"Look at this," Conrad said. On the far wall was a door with a padlock that looked exactly like the door at the end of the tunnel. Mark used the crowbar again but couldn't open the lock. Finally, the hinges gave way, and the kids pushed the door open a few inches.

"The passage," Conrad said.

Vicki explained how she and Conrad had walked the length of the tunnel. "It goes all the way to the river," she said.

"What do you think it's here for?" Shelly said.

"Somebody must have needed a quick

getaway," Conrad said, "but why would a school—"

Phoenix barked. The kids stared at one another. Mark ran up the stairs. Vicki heard a rumbling. Pieces from the leather Bible danced on the table in front of her.

Mark stuck his head back into the room and whispered, "Somebody's coming."

FIVE

The Visitor

"DON'T panic!" Vicki said. "They won't find us down here."

"I'll look through the hole in the tunnel and see who it is," Conrad said.

"Whoever it is, they sure are big," Charlie said. "Listen!"

The earth rumbled. Mark looked hard at Melinda. "Did you tip somebody?"

Melinda scowled. She looked at Vicki. "Is that what you think?"

"Tell us," Vicki said. "We need to know now."

Conrad returned, out of breath. "I can see a GC insignia on the side of the truck! I'm going back."

Melinda walked to the other side of the room, her head down.

Mark closed the doors leading to the basement and gently brought the trapdoor down on the secret passage. The rumbling increased.

Minutes passed. Finally, Vicki whispered, "Where's Conrad?"

Mark put a finger to his lips. His eyes darted. Footsteps above them. Doors opening. Voices.

"How could they have found us so fast?" Vicki said.

"Quick," Mark said, "everybody into the tunnel."

But it was too late. Vicki looked back and saw the trapdoor swing open.

The airstrip in Tel Aviv was a narrow lane of newly poured concrete. A woman in a brown jumpsuit approached and waved Taylor to a metal building. When they were inside the hangar, Taylor got out and hugged the woman.

"These are my friends," Taylor said, introducing Mr. Stein, Lionel, and Judd.

The woman was slender with dark hair and deep brown eyes. "Hasina Kamen," she said, extending a hand to each of them. She pushed a button and closed the hangar.

"I suppose you are all tired and hungry,"

Hasina said. She had a heavy Arabic accent, but she spoke English well. She led them into a conference area, where a tray of food was waiting.

"Is this who will paint your plane?" Mr. Stein said as he grabbed some pita bread and sauce.

"Hasina knows her stuff," Taylor said. "Max Stahley and I were working on a case in the Middle East when we met. I tried to get her to marry me."

Hasina blushed. "That is not the way I remember it."

Taylor laughed. "You can trust her with your life, which is what we're doing. Her dad was—"

Hasina held up a hand and asked Mr. Stein, "Why have you come to Tel Aviv with such a dangerous man?"

Mr. Stein explained that they were attending the Meeting of the Witnesses in Jerusalem. Hasina nodded. "There are many who have come in the last few days. Thousands. Do you consider yourselves followers of the rabbi?"

"Yes," Mr. Stein said. "Both Rabbi Ben-Judah and the rabbi named Jesus."

Hasina smiled. "Then you are no friend to the Global Community. Nicolae Carpathia has tried to postpone the conference many times."

"Dr. Ben-Judah will not stand for another delay," Mr. Stein said.

"There is a rumor that the potentate himself will make an appearance," Hasina said.

Taylor sat up straight. "Where'd you get that info?"

"Increased security at the largest airport in the city," Hasina said. "My sources say Carpathia will be here tomorrow."

"Why would Carpathia do that?" Taylor said.

Mr. Stein took more pita bread and smiled. "Perhaps he is on our side. Or he may foolishly think he can gain more followers."

"Tsion would never let Carpathia speak," Judd said.

"What if he's trying to kill the witnesses?" Lionel said.

"Where will you be staying?" Hasina said.

"God has brought us here by his own will," Mr. Stein said. "We are trusting him to provide."

"Your God will have to work a miracle if you hope to find hotel rooms," Hasina said. "Even Tel Aviv is booked."

Judd gave Mr. Stein a knowing look.

"Then we will have to pray," Mr. Stein said.

Hasina made a phone call and scheduled a driver. "You will stay here tonight. The driver will take you to Jerusalem in the morning."

Vicki watched the trapdoor open. Conrad stuck his head inside. At first, Vicki thought someone had forced him to betray the group. Then she saw a longhaired man with tattoos standing behind Conrad.

"Z!" Vicki shouted in relief.

Z knelt and peered into the dimly lit space. "Incredible." Then he laughed. "You guys don't have to hide from me. I use mouthwash."

Melinda pushed her way past Vicki and slammed the door at the top.

Vicki explained the situation to Z.

He frowned. "Having a GC Morale Monitor in your hideout's probably not the best idea I've heard all day. If she finds out who I am, that's worse."

"There wasn't much we could do," Vicki said. "I don't think she'll be a problem."

Mark scratched his head. "It's a pretty big risk."

Vicki rolled her eyes. *He's just like Judd,* she thought.

Vicki led the kids and Z upstairs. "What's that place down there?" she said.

"We've been looking for that a long time," Z said. "Let's unload and I'll tell you."

The kids eyed the huge truck parked in the front yard. On the side of the trailer was a Global Community insignia. Z explained that the gas station was nearly full of supplies. "My dad found this trailer a couple weeks ago. You should see everybody get outta the way when they see it coming."

"How'd you get past the logs in the driveway?" Conrad said.

Z pointed to the chains hanging on the front of the truck. "Took me a while, but I got through."

"What's in there?" Shelly said.

"Food mostly. And a couple surprises."

The kids spent the rest of the day unloading, organizing, and storing the canned food. They filled the storage area on the main floor and then moved to the basement. Z had them put water and fuel in the shed.

In the back of the truck, there was a stack of furniture. There were beds, mattresses, and even a kitchen table. Vicki was excited to see two couches. "I know exactly where those are going, but why did you take such a chance? Somebody could have followed you."

"I made sure they didn't," Z said. "The

truck not only has a Global Positioning System—you know, those satellite things that can show you which turn to make—it also has something like radar that helps me watch for cars behind me."

"You can tell if you're being tailed," Mark said.

"You got it," Z said. "Plus, I knew you guys could use the stuff. This is basically a trial run. If things go okay, I'll be back every few weeks. You'll need to figure out where to stash it all."

Conrad showed Z the generator. Z looked impressed. Melinda locked herself in her room. When evening came, they all ate heartily, then set up the couches in the room with the fireplace. They talked late into the night.

"What are you going to call this thing where you move food around the country?" Mark said.

"I have no idea," Z said. "I'm just getting the materials in place. Doesn't matter what we call it as long as it works. The way I figure it, there are believers all around the world who will need what we have. I just pray God brings the right people together."

"Tell us about the tunnel," Vicki said.

"Like I told you, this land's been in my family for years. The first house was built in the 1850s. The boarding school came along after that. My grandfather always said this was part of the Underground Railroad."

"Railroad tracks ran by here?" Charlie said.

"No," Darrion said. "I studied this. The Underground Railroad was a network of safe houses and paths that slaves used to escape."

"I didn't know Illinois was part of that," Shelly said.

"A lot of slaves from the deep South went through Ohio or Pennsylvania," Darrion said, "but a lot came through Illinois. Usually, the safe houses were near rivers—"

"Which has got to be why the tunnel ends near the water," Conrad said.

"My dad and I searched for hiding places," Z said. "We found a door in a wall upstairs that led down to that cellar, but we could never find any outside entrance."

"They must have hidden down there and escaped to the river," Vicki said.

Conrad pulled the piece of cloth from his pocket and handed it to Z. "I found this in the tunnel."

Z held the cloth like it was a work of art. "This looks like a dress for a rag doll. I always heard that women gathered to sew clothes for the runaways. They'd make dolls for the kids to make them feel better. One of the children must have dropped this on the way out."

The kids sat, stunned. Vicki thought of the brave men, women, and children who had been through the house, searching for freedom.

Finally, Z said, "My grandfather also told us he thought there was a safe hidden in or near the house. We never found it, but this makes me think he was probably right."

Early the next morning, Judd awoke and found Hasina in her office. Mr. Stein and Lionel agreed that someone should talk with her about God. Judd volunteered.

Hasina turned the volume of a news station down when Judd walked in. "Did you sleep well?"

Judd nodded. "I'm anxious to get to Jerusalem. And I'm curious. Did Taylor really ask you to marry him?"

Hasina smiled. Judd thought she looked a little sad. "Taylor Graham will never marry. I suppose I came as close as any woman ever has."

Silence followed. Judd bit his lip. "Taylor mentioned something about your father."

Hasina closed the book she was writing in

and sat back. She put both feet on the desk and looked squarely at Judd.

"I worshiped my father," Hasina said. "I was very young when my mother died. He could have shipped me off to any number of relatives, but he chose to keep me. He had great status as a pilot, but he gave that up to become a maintenance worker so he would have regular hours. He sacrificed everything for me."

"What happened?"

Hasina looked away. "Is *your* father still alive?"

"He was taken in the disappearances," Judd said.

"I'm sorry," Hasina said. "My father joined the Egyptian resistance. He helped plan the attack that led to World War III. He was shot down by Global Community planes near London. He called me the day before the bombings and told me he loved me. Over and over he said it. I never heard his voice again."

"And that's why you're against the GC?" Judd said.

"With every ounce of strength I have, I will avenge my father's death. That is what I live for."

Judd let the words sink in. After a few

moments he stammered as he tried to tell Hasina about God.

"Whatever it is, just say it," Hasina said.

"We're here for the meeting, and its purpose is to teach people to tell everyone how much God loves them. It would be awful if nobody talked with you about how much God cares for you."

Hasina smiled. "In the years before the disappearances, I worked as a guide in Israel. I came into contact with many Christians who tried to convince me of God's love."

"You didn't buy it?" Judd said.

Hasina shook her head. "I have seen the meteors, felt the earthquake. Most of my friends are dead. Whether there is a God of love out there somewhere, I do not know. I have never seen him. But I know you are against Nicolae Carpathia." Hasina looked at Judd without blinking. "Never get in my way. I will not rest, and I will let no one keep me from the sacred pledge of avenging my father's death."

Vicki was tired. She handed Z a pillow and some blankets.

"That's okay," Z said. "I sleep in the truck. Probably more comfortable anyway."

Mark said, "What about the surprise?"

Z stood and headed for the kitchen. In the doorway he turned. "How do you keep up with the news?"

"We don't have a TV," Mark said. "We get some stations on the Internet. That's our main link to the outside world."

Z returned with two boxes. As he opened the first, he said, "I got to thinking about the meeting and how much you will want to see what's going on." Z pulled out an ultrathin computer. "This oughta be faster and more powerful than what you have."

"The screen is so big!" Shelly said.

"Got it from a GC shipment. It's connected to the Internet by satellite. You don't have to dial up anything. Just turn it on and you're connected. And the best thing is, it's secure. The Global Community can't trace it."

"How'd you get it?" Mark said.

"Can't tell you," Z said. He pulled out a smaller box and handed it to him. "This is the phone that goes with it. It's hooked up to Carpathia's Cell-Sol system. They can't trace it. You should be able to keep in touch with the outside world. And the best thing is, they pick up the tab."

The kids laughed.

Shelly rushed into the room and grabbed Vicki. "Come quick! Melinda's gone."

SIX

Confession

VICKI rushed to Melinda's room. Cool air blew through the open window. Vicki grabbed Phoenix by the collar and let him sniff at the blankets. "Go get her, boy!"

Phoenix jumped through the window and bounded across the wooden walkway. Vicki followed. Phoenix headed toward the road, then turned and ran into the woods.

Mark caught up to Vicki. "If she gets away—"

"Let me handle this," Vicki said.

Mark threw both hands in the air. "I was just trying to help."

Vicki looked for Phoenix. He sniffed and ran through leaves in the distance. Someone whimpered. Vicki found Melinda near Felicia's grave. Phoenix licked the girl's hand. Vicki sat beside her.

Melinda spoke through tears. "When you heard that truck, you assumed I had told someone. I can't stay here."

"I'm sorry," Vicki said. "Mark thought you'd alerted the GC."

"You did too! Admit it."

"I don't know what I thought," Vicki said.

"I have to get out of here. I can't live with you people."

Conrad ran up the hill. Vicki waved him away.

"Who's the guy with the truck?" Melinda said.

"A friend with supplies," Vicki said.

Melinda started to leave, but Vicki grabbed her arm. "It's not going to be easy for us, but we have to admit we need each other."

Melinda wiped her eyes and stared at Vicki. "What do you mean?"

"We need you to keep quiet about us, and you need us for protection. From the GC and the judgments on the way."

"Protect me?"

"We saved you from the poisoned water," Vicki said. "I just wish we could have gotten to Felicia before she drank it."

"I'm out of place," Melinda said. "I feel guilty for staying with you and not turning you in. At the same time . . ." Melinda's voice trailed off.

"What?" Vicki said.

"There's something I haven't told you."

Judd tried to talk more with Hasina, but her hatred for the Global Community kept her from listening. Lionel rushed in. "You should see this."

Mr. Stein watched a report about Nicolae Carpathia. The news conference was held at the main airport in Tel Aviv. Leon Fortunato, Carpathia's right-hand man, stood dutifully in the background as Enigma Babylon's Peter Mathews introduced the potentate.

"I cannot tell you what a pleasure it is to be back in Israel," Carpathia said with a broad smile. "I am eager to welcome the devotees of Dr. Ben-Judah and to display the openness of the Global Community to diverse opinion and belief."

"Right," Judd said sarcastically.

"I am pleased to reaffirm my guarantee of safety to the rabbi and the thousands of visitors from all over the world," Carpathia continued. "I will withhold further comment, assuming I will be welcome to address the honored assembly within the next few days."

"Surely Tsion won't let him," Judd said.

Mr. Stein stroked the stubbly beard he had

grown. "I'm wondering how the witnesses will respond."

"The people in the stadium?" Lionel said.

"Eli and Moishe," Mr. Stein said.

Taylor Graham walked into the room and flipped off the television. "You guys want a little company at that meeting of yours? I hear the big guy is making an appearance."

Judd knew from reading Tsion's views of the book of Revelation that Nicolae Carpathia would be killed. But Judd thought it was too soon. They had just passed the two-year mark of the beginning of the Tribulation, and from what Judd could remember, Nicolae wasn't supposed to die for another year and a half.

While Lionel and Mr. Stein talked with Taylor, Judd slipped into Hasina's empty office and pulled up Tsion's Web site. Judd gasped when he saw Tsion's travel schedule. Everyone, including the Global Community, could see it!

Between Tsion's directions to the witnesses and what Buck Williams wrote in his Web magazine, *The Truth*, Judd couldn't wait for the meeting to begin. One thing was sure. Buck's days as the editor of Nicolae Carpathia's global magazine were over. Judd wondered whether Buck would attend the conference with Tsion or play it safe.

Later, a car pulled up outside. Judd and the others thanked Hasina for her kindness. "Perhaps I'll see you before you leave?" she said.

The drive to Jerusalem went quickly. Judd pointed out some of the historical sites as they drew closer. It was as if they had gone through a time warp. Tel Aviv was modern and fast paced. But as they neared the old city of Jerusalem, it looked thousands of years old. Mr. Stein watched in amazement. "I feel God has me here for a reason."

Tens of thousands crowded the streets. Many were no doubt converted Jewish witnesses from around the world.

"Can you drive us by the Temple Mount?" Mr. Stein said.

The driver wound his way through the jammed streets. "You should see it at night," the driver said. "It is spectacular."

The new temple gleamed in the morning sun. The Global Community had spent millions creating this structure to honor Nicolae Carpathia. Judd figured when the Dome of the Rock was moved to New Babylon, animal sacrifices wouldn't be far behind. He was right. Peter the Second had welcomed the Orthodox Jews into the Enigma Babylon faith. Tsion Ben-Judah wrote in disgust about the structure. He said the new building and the sacrifices were an affront to the true God of Israel.

The driver of the car turned and, in a heavy Israeli accent, said, "I will not be able to get you close to Teddy Kollek Stadium. Too many people."

"We can walk," Mr. Stein said. "We are looking for a room for the week. Can you help?"

The driver shook his head. "If you do not have a place to stay, may God help you."

Mr. Stein smiled. "He will."

Mr. Stein paid the driver, and the three began their walk.

"Who is Teddy Kollek, anyway?" Lionel said.

"I believe he was the mayor of Jerusalem for many years," Mr. Stein said. "He helped develop the city."

"How many people will the stadium hold?" Lionel said.

Mr. Stein looked around. "Not this many. Tsion's Web site said they would transmit the signal to other areas, but I must be where Dr. Ben-Judah is."

Global Community guards patrolled the area around the stadium. "The meeting starts tomorrow night," a guard said. "Come back then."

Judd pointed out several hotels as they

continued, but all were booked. Mr. Stein pleaded with manager after manager, offering several times the amount of a single room. Each time, they were turned away.

"Does it strike you funny that there's no room at any of these inns?" Lionel said with a smile.

Melinda sat like a statue next to Felicia's grave.

"You want to go inside?" Vicki said. "It's late, and really cold."

"You asked about my mother," Melinda said.

"I figured you didn't want to talk about her," Vicki said.

"I didn't. But now . . ."

"What is it?"

Melinda took a deep breath. "My mom believed what you do."

Vicki couldn't speak.

"Not always. She used to be as wild as my dad. Even wilder. They'd go to cocktail parties and come home blasted. When my dad was on the road, she'd sneak out. She thought I didn't see her. I never told my dad, but I saw.

"I was out late one night. I came home and found her crying in the living room. There was a woman with her. We called her the preacher lady. She said my mother had something to tell me.

"I thought my mom had gotten some kind of disease the way she was crying. But that wasn't it. She said she was sorry for being a bad mother.

"Then the preacher lady said my mom had just asked Jesus to forgive her. I couldn't believe it. I'd heard this Jesus talk from a couple of kids at school. I thought it was trash."

"What happened?" Vicki said.

"I told her I didn't want to hear it. She said she'd waited up all night to talk with me. My dad had been there and left. I started up the stairs, and my mom followed. When I got to the top, she grabbed me by the arm. She begged me to listen."

Melinda closed her eyes, as if she were watching the scene again. "I yelled something awful at her and pulled away. When I did, she lost her balance. I turned around. There was nothing I could do. She fell the whole way down those stairs.

"The preacher lady rushed to her and felt her neck. She ran for the phone. I flew down the stairs to see if I could help. Honestly, I didn't mean to hurt her."

Vicki nodded. "Was she dead when you got there?"

Melinda stared at Felicia's grave. "All that was left at the bottom of the stairs were her dress and shoes. I screamed and ran for the preacher lady. The phone was hanging by the cord. Her clothes were in a pile on the floor."

"You must have been so scared," Vicki said.

"I thought I'd killed her," Melinda said. "Killed them both."

"Why did you tell me this story?" Vicki said.

"I've tried to get it out of my head for so long. I didn't even tell my dad about it for a long time. When I did, he said I was crazy. Accused me of being drunk." Melinda sighed. "The way you looked at me tonight when you said you were sorry, it reminded me of my mom."

Vicki put an arm around Melinda. "If you want, I'll tell you exactly what happened to your mom."

When evening came and they still hadn't found a place to stay, Judd suggested they go back to the Temple Mount. "A lot of people stay there through the night."

"We can see the witnesses," Mr. Stein said, "Eli and Moishe!"

Mr. Stein darted into a store and brought back three heavy blankets. "These will keep us warm."

Judd hailed a cab. He recalled the terror the two witnesses had created the last time he had seen them.

A crowd gathered to watch Eli and Moishe thirty feet from the wrought-iron fence. Eli sat Indian style, his back to a stone wall. A slight breeze sent a chill through Judd and moved Eli's long hair and beard, but the prophet was unmoving, unblinking. Moishe stood near the fence, staring at the crowd.

"When's the show start?" a young man said, giggling, from the back of the crowd.

"Yeah, say something," another said.

"Come with me," Judd said. He led Mr. Stein and Lionel to a ledge overlooking the witnesses. Bushes blocked their view of the crowd.

"This will be a good place to rest," Mr. Stein said. They spread out their blankets and sat.

"I've seen them talk without moving their mouths," Judd said. "Everybody understands in his own language." Judd was exhausted. He put his head down and fell asleep.

Lionel shook him awake some time later. "Something's going on."

Judd rubbed his eyes and peered through

the bushes. A disturbance in the crowd had caused some to back away from the fence.

"Carpathia!" someone shouted. "It's the potentate!"

"I don't believe it," Lionel said. "Those guys will eat him alive."

Judd recognized Leon Fortunato, Carpathia's right-hand man. He instructed the guards to keep the crowd away. The potentate boldly moved within ten feet of the fence. Someone shouted a greeting. Carpathia held a finger to his lips, and the crowd grew quiet.

The silence was shattered by the booming voice of Moishe. "Woe unto the enemy of the Most High God!"

Carpathia seemed startled but quickly collected himself. He smiled and spoke softly. "I am hardly the enemy of God. Many say I *am* the Most High God."

Moishe crossed his arms over his chest and spoke softly to Carpathia.

"What did he say?" Lionel said.

"I couldn't tell," Mr. Stein said.

Now Carpathia clenched his teeth and said, "Let me tell you and your companion something. You have persecuted Israel long enough with the drought and the water turned to blood. You will lift your hocus-pocus or live to regret it."

It was Eli's turn. He motioned Nicolae closer and spoke with great volume. Judd recoiled in fear. "Until the due time, you have no authority over the lampstands of God Almighty!" Eli said.

Carpathia seethed. "We shall see who will win in the end."

Eli stared at Carpathia. "Who will win in the end was determined before the beginning of time. Lo, the poison you inflict on the earth shall rot you from within for eternity."

Carpathia stepped back. He smiled. "I warn you to stay away from the charade of the so-called saints. I have guaranteed their safety, not yours."

Eli and Moishe spoke in unison. "He and she who have ears, let them hear. We are bound neither by time nor space, and those who shall benefit by our presence and testimony stand within the sound of our proclamation."

Leon Fortunato and the guards ushered the potentate away from the area. Mr. Stein was about to speak when someone moved back through the bushes. When it was clear they were safe, Lionel spoke.

"I got everything except the last statement," Lionel said. "What was all that 'benefit by our presence' jazz?"

Mr. Stein shrugged and looked at Judd.

"I don't know either," Judd said, "but this is the first time I've ever heard them say, 'He *and she* who have ears, let them hear.'"

SEVEN

The Surprise Meeting

VICKI took Melinda to the house and told her own story. Vicki's parents had changed overnight. They wanted Vicki to attend church, but Vicki wouldn't. Then came the awful morning when Vicki realized her whole family had disappeared.

"Would you let me show you verses from the Bible?"

Melinda frowned. "Don't think I'm ready for that."

Someone knocked on Melinda's door. "Can I see you a minute, Vicki?" Mark said.

"I'm kind of in the middle of something—"

"It's important."

"Go ahead," Melinda said. "I'm tired. We can talk tomorrow."

Vicki joined Mark in the kitchen. The others had gone to bed.

"We had a meeting while you were out looking for her," Mark said, "and most of us think it's time to set some rules about who gets to stay."

"Most of us?" Vicki said.

Mark shrugged. "Darrion and Conrad think I—*we* might be going a little too far."

"What do you propose?" Vicki said.

"If this is going to be a training ground for the Young Trib Force," Mark said, "the people who stay here ought to have the mark of the believer. If they don't, we can't trust them."

"Melinda just told me—"

"I'm not talking about just Melinda," Mark said. "Charlie's a threat to us too."

"How?"

"He could walk out of here any time he wanted," Mark said. "Even if he doesn't mean to, he could bring trouble."

Vicki held up a hand. "I understand about safety. I don't want the GC to find us any more than you do, but for some reason, God brought three people here who aren't believers. One of them is buried up on the hill. I don't want the same thing to happen to the other two."

"That's not the point," Mark said.

"It is the point," Vicki said.

"Then this isn't the place for me," Mark said.

Vicki sat, exhausted. She thought her troubles with the group were over when Judd had left. "Can we talk about this in the morning?" she said.

Judd, Lionel, and Mr. Stein slept near the witnesses until Global Community guards found them and shooed them away. They spent the rest of the night wandering the streets of the old city. Before dawn, Mr. Stein led them through a gate and past a cemetery. They found a peaceful place to watch the sunrise. Judd asked Mr. Stein what they were going to do, but the man didn't seem upset. As they drank the last of their water, Lionel wandered off. A few minutes later, he returned.

"Do you guys know what this place is?" Lionel said. "It's the Garden of Gethsemane. This is where Jesus was betrayed. Where he prayed on the night of his arrest."

Mr. Stein looked around the garden in awe.

A man approached. He was short, with stooped shoulders. He wore a wide-brimmed hat that hid his eyes. With a powerful voice he said to Mr. Stein, "Are you one of the witnesses?"

Judd put a hand on Mr. Stein's shoulder.

Being in Israel didn't mean they were out of danger.

"Why do you ask?"

"Are you one of those called by God?" the man said. He drew close and lifted his hat above his forehead. Judd saw the telltale mark of the believer.

"I can see it in your eyes," the man said. "You have the fire of God in you."

"Are you a witness?" Lionel said.

The man turned and motioned for them to follow him.

"Where are you taking us?" Judd said.

"Where you are supposed to be," the man said.

Mr. Stein followed. Judd hesitated. Lionel shrugged, and they jogged to catch up. The man's car was parked a few blocks away. The three squeezed into the tiny backseat.

"Where are we going?" Mr. Stein said.

"You will see. When did you get to Israel?"

Mr. Stein told him when they had arrived and that they had slept outside the previous night.

"The foxes have holes," the man said, shaking his head. "You will not sleep outside again."

The man wound past the old city and into a newer section. The streets were already congested with traffic and people on foot.

The man pointed out the Knesset, Israel's Parliament.

Mr. Stein introduced himself, then Judd and Lionel. "What is your name?"

"I am Yitzhak Weizmann, and God told me to expect you."

Mr. Stein looked at Judd and Lionel. "What do you mean?"

"The Lord God of Israel impressed upon me to make room for you. I have done as he suggested."

"God spoke to you and told you we would be coming?" Judd said, his mouth open.

Yitzhak ignored the question. They drove near Teddy Kollek Stadium. "That is where you will be tonight, along with thousands of other witnesses. I cannot wait until the rabbi speaks. I was watching the day he announced his findings on television."

They stopped in a huge parking lot near what looked like a school. "This is Hebrew University," Yitzhak said. "You are in the building on the far side. You will be able to walk to the stadium tonight." Yitzhak laughed. "If you leave early enough."

Yitzhak led them along a concrete path to a back entrance. Before he opened the door he said, "In the name of Jesus, our Lord and

Savior, our provider, I welcome you." He opened the door.

What Judd saw next would stay with him the rest of his life. The gymnasium had been transformed into an emergency shelter for witnesses. Hundreds of cots filled the room. People gathered in small groups to pray. Others ate sack lunches and watched one of several monitors positioned throughout the room.

"Incredible," Judd said.

Yitzhak smiled. "When I read Tsion's messages about the meeting, God gave me this idea. I knew there would not be enough room in hotels for all of the witnesses, so I approached the administration of the university. They allowed me to rent five buildings like this."

"And they knew what you were using them for?" Mr. Stein said.

"They only know that I was willing to pay twice what they are worth," Yitzhak said, smiling.

"So you didn't really know *we* were coming," Judd said.

"Our God knows the number of hairs on your head. This morning I have found fourteen witnesses who spent the night sleeping on the ground. I must look for more."

Yitzhak showed them where to register for

a cot. Mr. Stein asked the cost. "The money
has already been paid," Yitzhak said. "Enjoy
your stay."

Yitzhak left them, and they spent the rest
of the morning meeting other witnesses and
sharing stories. Mr. Stein couldn't stop talking. He went from one person to the next,
trying to find out more about how to spread
their message.

Judd and Lionel found their cots and
collapsed.

Vicki awoke the next morning with a pain in
her stomach. She felt such pressure to hold
everything together. She stared at the ceiling
and listened to the sounds coming from the
kitchen. The kids were saying good-bye to Z.

Vicki dressed quickly and ran to the truck.

"Sounds like you had an interesting night,"
Z said.

Vicki got into the truck and closed the
door. "This seemed so perfect for us, but
even all the way out here we don't feel safe."

Z scratched his head. "Here's what I know.
God wanted you here. That's pretty clear,
right?"

Vicki nodded.

"If you know that, you know he's gonna
work out the rest."

"I just don't know what to do. . . ."

Z started the big rig, and the whole truck shook. "I put a box for you in the kitchen. Hang on to your dream and don't give up."

Vicki and the others watched Z drive off. Conrad and Mark helped with the logs at the end of the road. Vicki looked in on Melinda, but she was still asleep.

When they were all gathered, Vicki asked Charlie to take Phoenix outside. Vicki briefly explained Melinda's story. "We can pull together on this, or we can pull apart. But I don't think we're as strong if we split up.

"God's given us this place. With the Meeting of the Witnesses starting, I think we should use this next week to study and pray that God would use us how he wants."

No one spoke. Vicki looked at each person and recalled what they had been through together. Though Mark was outspoken, she knew he loved God and wanted to do the right thing. Shelly had been with her almost from the start. Darrion had seen so much loss, she looked like a shell.

Finally, Conrad spoke. "None of us knows how much longer we have. I think Vicki's right. If we can help people like Melinda and

Charlie know the truth, I think we ought to do it."

"There's risk in everything," Shelly said. "I say we open the place up and let God bring whoever he wants, believer or not."

Everyone spoke in support of Vicki except Mark. He stared at the floor. "I lost a lot of friends when the Global Community attacked the militia base. Now I've lost my cousin, John. Ryan's gone. Chaya's gone. The people we knew at the church. I don't want to hold you guys back. Maybe if I take some time . . ."

Mark's voice trailed off. Vicki could tell he was hurting.

"I'm thinking of going back to find my aunt," Mark said. "She'll want to know about John. She's the last of my family, as far as I know."

"There are two cycles left," Conrad said. "Take one."

"How will you see the Meeting of the Witnesses?" Vicki said.

"Can I take Judd's laptop?"

Vicki nodded.

Mark gathered some supplies later that morning. He said good-bye to everyone. When he got to Vicki, she said, "I hope you'll come back."

Mark pursed his lips. "Yeah."

When Judd awoke that afternoon, the room was crowded with witnesses. People stood shoulder to shoulder around Judd's cot. Judd stood on his cot. Lionel did the same.

A deep-voiced man spoke through a megaphone at the front of the gym. Judd recognized the hat and the stooped shoulders. It was Yitzhak. He stood on a stepladder and spoke in Hebrew, then translated into English. Around the room small groups who spoke other languages gathered for the translation.

"Last night, I met with others in the local committee for a final walk-through of the program," Yitzhak said. "You will be happy to know that Tsion Ben-Judah is here and alive and well!"

A cheer went up from the group. Some shouted, "May God be praised!" Others spoke in their own languages.

A chill went down Judd's spine. *This is what heaven is going to be like*, he thought.

When the cheering died down, Yitzhak said, "But there has been a disturbing development. The reports we have heard have been confirmed. Nicolae Carpathia has asked to address the meeting tonight."

A murmur rose from the crowd. Yitzhak held up a hand. "I do not know whether Dr.

Ben-Judah will allow it, or if he refuses what will happen. But I do know that God is in control of this meeting!"

Another cheer arose.

"And now, I urge you to pray with me. What we will learn over the next few days will be vital. But our hearts must be right."

For the next fifteen minutes, Judd heard the sound of voices praying in different languages. Yitzhak gently interrupted them by saying, "My friends, there will be some in the stadium and many watching and listening via satellite who do not know our Messiah. Let us pray earnestly for God to open their eyes."

Again, voices swirled in prayer. Judd moved toward Lionel. "Can you believe this?"

Lionel shook his head.

As the prayers of the people wound down, Yitzhak said, "In the spirit of these prayers, O God, we commit ourselves to you. We ask that you give us clear minds to understand your teaching. In Jesus' name, amen."

Yitzhak led the group out the back door. There was no shoving, no pushing, no trying to get the best spot in line. Everyone slowly followed the little man across the parking lot toward the stadium.

"Where's Mr. Stein?" Lionel said.

Judd shrugged. "I guess we'll find him later."

Judd had never seen such traffic. Every road to the stadium was jammed with cars and pedestrians. Every person he saw seemed happy. People carried satchels and note-books and water bottles. Most of those on foot made it to the stadium faster than those in cars and buses.

"This looks like a lot more people than that stadium could ever hold," Lionel said.

Judd saw two jeeps with flashing yellow lights. Each vehicle carried four armed Global Community guards. Between the jeeps was a Mercedes van. Someone shouted, "The rabbi!"

With that, people broke from the line and rushed to the van. They waved and shouted and joyfully pounded on the doors and windows. Judd and Lionel tried to get close, but they were pushed back by the trailing GC jeep.

Suddenly, the van cut to the left and flew toward the median. The GC vehicles fol-lowed, blowing their sirens and bouncing crazily behind the van.

When they made it to the stadium, Judd noticed monitors outside the stadium for those who couldn't get in. Judd and Lionel squeezed their way through the crowd. Judd remembered his first trip to Wrigley Field with his dad and the sight of the green grass and white lines and the ivy on the outfield wall. It had filled him with awe. That was nothing compared to this. Men and women from around the world filled the stands and the infield. They shouted praises to God in many languages. Some huddled in groups to pray. Others sang and swayed as they wrapped their arms around each other.

A line of people appeared through an opening at the back of the stage. "Interpreters," Lionel whispered. The crowd grew quiet.

At exactly seven, a man strode to a simple wood lectern and said, "Welcome, my brothers and sisters, in the name of the Lord God Almighty. . . ."

EIGHT

Witnesses to History

JUDD felt a chill down his spine. Before the translators could speak, the stadium erupted in cheering. When the applause faded, the man at the podium nodded to the interpreters, but the crowd shouted, *"Nein!"* *"Nyet!"*

"What's going on?" Lionel said.

The man continued. ". . . maker of heaven and earth . . . and his Son, Jesus Christ, the Messiah!"

The crowd went wild again. Someone hurried onto the stage. Judd leaned close to Lionel. "I think the same thing that happened at the Wailing Wall is happening here."

"What do you mean?"

"Everybody understands in their own language," Judd said. "They don't need the interpreters. That's why everybody's shouting no!"

The translators walked away from their

positions. The crowd thundered. The man held up his hands and asked them to pray.

Many knelt in front of their seats. "Father, we are grateful for having been spared by your grace and love," the man prayed. "You are indeed the God of new beginnings and second chances. We are about to hear from our beloved rabbi, and our prayer is that you would supernaturally prepare our hearts and minds to absorb everything you have given him to say. We pray this in the matchless name of the King of kings and Lord of lords. Amen."

A huge "Amen!" echoed through the stadium. The massive congregation began to sing, "Amazing grace! how sweet the sound— that saved a wretch like me! I once was lost but now am found, was blind but now I see."

Judd remembered his mother singing that song. He had hated it because he didn't think he was such a bad person. But now, knowing the truth about himself and what God had done, Judd choked through the words. The sound of twenty-five thousand believers singing from their hearts, plus the thousands outside joining in, overwhelmed him.

"When we've been there ten thousand years, bright shining as the sun, we've no less days to sing God's praise than when we'd first begun."

The man at the podium asked the crowd to sit. "The vast majority of us know our speaker tonight only as a name on our computer screens," he began. "It is my honor—"

Before he could finish, people rose to their feet as one, cheering, clapping, shouting, whistling. Tsion Ben-Judah was nudged from the edge of the stage. He hesitated, looking embarrassed. The noise was deafening. Finally, the crowd settled.

"My beloved brothers and sisters, I accept your warm greeting in the name that is above all names. All glory and honor is due the triune God." As the crowd began to respond again, Tsion quickly asked that they withhold their praise until the end of the teaching.

Vicki and the others gathered in a meeting room to watch the opening session at 11:00 A.M. their time. After Mark had left, Vicki found Z's box in the kitchen. Inside was a note. "Every school needs supplies. I hope these help."

Underneath was a huge stack of spiral notebooks, pens, colored pencils, and other materials. Vicki handed out the notebooks before Tsion began his message. "Z thought of everything," Vicki said.

Tsion's voice filled the room. "Ladies and gentlemen," he said, leaning over his notes, "never in my life have I been more eager to share a message from the Word of God. I stand before you with the unique privilege, I believe, of speaking to many of the 144,000 witnesses prophesied in the Scriptures."

The camera panned the crowd. Vicki was overcome by the size of the gathering and the anxious faces of people who hung on Tsion's every word.

"Let me review the basics of God's plan of salvation so we may soon leave this place and get back to the work to which he has called us. You have each been assigned a location for all-day training tomorrow and the next day. On both nights we will meet back here for encouragement and fellowship and teaching."

Tsion outlined the evidence from the Old Testament proving Jesus was the Messiah. He recited the many names of God and finished with the powerful passage from Isaiah 9:6: "For unto us a Child is born, unto us a Son is given; and the government will be upon His shoulder. And His name will be called Wonderful, Counselor, Mighty God, Everlasting Father, Prince of Peace."

The crowd could not contain itself, leaping to its feet. Tsion smiled and encouraged them. "Jesus himself said that if we do not glorify God, the very stones would have to cry out."

Cheers went up around the room. Vicki

jotted something down in her notebook. Someone moved near the doorway. It was Melinda. "What's going on?" she said.

"We're watching the opening session," Vicki said, as the kids fell silent. "Watch with us."

Melinda stepped back. "I don't want to interrupt."

"Please," Vicki said. "It might be good for you to hear it from a different perspective."

Conrad stood and offered Melinda his chair. She shook her head and stood in the back.

Tsion walked through God's plan from the beginning of time, showing that Jesus was sent as the spotless lamb, a sacrifice to take away the sins of the world.

"We are sinful from the day we are born and because God is holy, there is nothing we can do to restore that relationship. God had to restore it himself. That is why Christ died. Anyone who accepts the fact that they are a sinner and Christ died for them can be born again spiritually into eternal life.

"In John 14:6, Jesus himself said he was the way, the truth, and the life, and that no man can come to the Father except through him. This is our message to the nations. This is our message to the desperate, the sick, the terrified."

Vicki glanced at Melinda. The girl was deep in thought.

Tsion continued. "There should be no doubt in anyone's mind—even those who have chosen to live in opposition to God—that he is real and that a person is either for him or against him. We should have the boldness of Christ to aggressively tell the world of its only hope in him.

"The bottom line is that we have been called as his divine witnesses—144,000 strong—through whom he has begun a great soul harvest. This will result in what John the Revelator calls 'a great multitude which no one could number.' Before you fall asleep tonight, read Revelation 7 and thrill with me to the description of the harvest you and I have been called to reap."

Vicki turned to Revelation 7 and read along as Tsion spoke. "John says it is made up of souls from all nations, kindreds, peoples, tribes, and tongues. One day they will stand before his throne and before the Lamb, clothed with white robes and carrying palms in their hands!"

Judd rose with the crowd at Teddy Kollek Stadium as Tsion's voice thundered. "They will cry with a loud voice, saying, 'Salvation belongs to our God who sits on the throne, and to the Lamb.'

"The angels around the throne will fall on their faces and worship God, saying, 'Amen! Blessing and glory and wisdom, thanksgiving and honor and power and might, be to our God forever and ever. Amen.'" Tsion stepped back.

The crowd roared. Judd was overwhelmed. He leaned forward, trying to picture that scene. He saw that Tsion had moved back to the microphone. The standing thousands quieted again, as if desperate to catch every word.

"John was asked by one of the elders at the throne, 'Who are these arrayed in white robes, and where did they come from?' And John said, 'Sir, you know.' And the elder said, 'These are the ones who come out of the great tribulation, and washed their robes and made them white in the blood of the Lamb.'"

Tsion waited for another cheer to subside, then continued: "'They shall neither hunger anymore nor thirst anymore.' The Lamb himself shall feed them and lead them to fountains of living water. And, best of all, my dear family, God shall wipe away all tears from their eyes."

Tsion raised a hand before they could cheer again. "We shall be here in Israel two more full days and nights, preparing for battle. Put aside fear! Put on boldness! Were you surprised that all of us, each and every one, were spared the last few judgments I wrote about? When the rain and hail and fire came from the sky and the meteors scorched a third of the plant life and poisoned a third of the waters of the world, how was it that we escaped? Luck? Chance?"

The crowd shouted, "No!"

"No!" Tsion echoed. "The Scriptures say that an angel ascending from the east, having the seal of the living God, cried with a loud voice to the four angels to whom it was given to hurt the earth and the sea. And what did he tell them? He said, 'Do not harm the earth, the sea, or the trees till we have sealed the servants of our God on their foreheads.' And John writes, 'I heard the number of those who were sealed. One hundred and forty-four thousand of all the tribes of the children of Israel were sealed.'"

Vicki and the others jotted notes furiously. It felt good to study again. Tsion's words were like water on dry ground. Vicki knew people around the world were watching this very meeting.

Tsion moved close to the microphone and

spoke softly. "And now let me close by reminding you that the bedrock of our faith remains the verse our Gentile brothers and sisters have so cherished from the beginning. John 3:16 says, 'For God so loved the world that He gave His only—'"

Tsion stopped talking. Vicki leaned forward. There was a faint noise coming from the speakers. She turned to the doorway and noticed Melinda was gone.

Judd heard the rumble behind them and turned. A helicopter slowly came into view over the lights of the stadium. The *thwock thwock thwock* of the gleaming white helicopter drew every eye. Tsion stepped back from the podium and lowered his head, as if in prayer.

Judd recognized the GC insignia on the side of the chopper as it slowly descended. The wind whipped Tsion's hair and clothes.

"Is that who I think it is?" Lionel said.

"I'm afraid so," Judd said, staring at the chopper as the engine shuddered and stopped. A murmur rose from the crowd as Leon Fortunato bounded from the craft to the lectern. He nodded to Tsion, who did not respond. "Dr. Ben-Judah, local and international organizing committee, and assembled guests," he said loudly.

Thousands murmured in different languages. Finally, Judd understood. "Translators," Judd said to Lionel. "They need translators to understand Fortunato!"

Someone in front repeated what Judd had said at the top of his lungs. Others shrugged, looked puzzled, and began jabbering.

Fortunato looked at Tsion. "Dr. Ben-Judah, is there someone who can translate?"

Tsion did not look at him.

Fortunato then called for the interpreters to come forward. Judd stretched to see the interpreters who sat near the front row on the infield. They looked to Tsion, but Tsion stared straight ahead.

"Please," Fortunato continued, "it isn't fair that only those who understand English may enjoy the remarks of your next two hosts."

"*Two* hosts?" Lionel said. "Who else is with Carpathia?"

Tsion raised his head slightly. The interpreters hurried to their microphones. Fortunato apparently expected applause when he mentioned Nicolae Carpathia's name, but no one moved. Fortunato cleared his throat and said, "First, I would like to introduce the revered head of the new Enigma Babylon One World Faith, the supreme pontiff, Pontifex Maximus, Peter the Second!"

Judd looked at Lionel and raised an eyebrow.

"They've got to be out of their minds, bringing him here," Lionel said.

Judd knew this was the former archbishop of Cincinnati, Peter Mathews. He was now the head of a mixture of nearly every religion on the globe except for Judaism and Christianity.

Peter the Second stepped out of the helicopter in an outfit that surprised even Judd. He wore a huge, pointed hat and a long, yellow robe with puffy sleeves. Several garments, inlaid with brightly colored stones, draped over his body. The supreme pontiff lifted his hands in a circle as if to bless everyone. When he turned to bless the people sitting behind him, Judd saw signs of the zodiac on the back of his robe.

"Looks like he wore the wrapping paper from his Christmas presents," Lionel said.

Peter stretched out his arms and spoke dramatically. "My blessed brothers and sisters in the pursuit of higher consciousness, it warms my heart to see all of you here, studying under my colleague, Dr. Tsion Ben Judah!"

Peter waited for the applause and cheers. None came.

"I confer upon this gathering the blessings of the universal father and mother and animal deities who lovingly guide us on our path to true spirituality. In the spirit of harmony, I appeal to Dr. Ben-Judah and others in your leadership to join Enigma Babylon One World Faith, where we affirm and accept the beliefs of all the world's great religions."

The stadium was deathly silent. Fortunato announced, "And now it gives me pleasure to introduce the man who has united the world into one global community, His Excellency and your potentate, Nicolae Carpathia! Would you rise as he comes with a word of greeting."

No one stood. Lionel whispered into Judd's ear, "Nicolae's always been able to win over his audience. Think he'll be able to do that here?"

Carpathia appeared on the steps of the helicopter, a frozen smile etched on his face. He nodded toward Fortunato and Peter the Second.

Someone moved to Judd's right. A man was making his way along a back wall of the stadium. Lionel saw him too and slipped out. Just before Carpathia made it to the microphone, Lionel returned.

"You're not going to believe this," Lionel said. "That's Taylor Graham!"

NINE

Nicolae's Speech

As Nicolae Carpathia stepped to the podium, Judd slipped from his seat. "If I'm not back before this ends, stay here," Judd said to Lionel. Taylor Graham was still moving when Judd caught up to him.

"What are you doing?" Judd whispered.

Taylor whirled, ready to fight. When he recognized Judd, he rolled his eyes and put a finger to his lips. "I came to hear Carpathia."

"Fellow citizens of the Global Community," Carpathia began, "as your potentate, I welcome you to Israel and to this great arena, named after a man of the past, a man of peace and harmony and statesmanship."

Judd knew what Nicolae was doing. He was trying to win the crowd by talking about a well-known Israeli. Judd tried to talk with Taylor, but he motioned for Judd to keep quiet. An armed Global Community guard

approached them. "Take it outside," he said
sternly.

Judd nodded. Taylor followed Judd
through the gate.

Vicki couldn't believe Nicolae Carpathia
would interrupt the Meeting of the Witnesses.
The kids groaned when they saw him arrive.

"Do we have to watch this?" Shelly said.

"He's going to schmooze them all he can,"
Conrad said.

Carpathia pledged his protection and
support of those who followed the teachings
of Dr. Ben-Judah. "As a famous teacher of
Israel once said, 'Blessed are the peacemak-
ers, for they shall be called sons of God.'"

Carpathia paused. When the stadium
remained silent, he said, "We in the Global
Community wish this kind of peace, not as a
slogan, but as a living reality."

Vicki turned. Melinda stood in the doorway again, listening.

Judd and Taylor walked away from the stadium. They could still see the huge monitors
and hear Carpathia's powerful voice.

"Why did you come here?" Judd said.

"You know why," Taylor said. "Saint Nick."

"You're not thinking of—"

"Only a fool would try to get a weapon past those guards." Taylor smiled. "I just wanted to make sure that was Nick in the white chopper."

Taylor opened the trunk of his car. He put on a Global Community uniform and zipped it quickly. "This is where you check out, okay?"

"Don't do this," Judd said.

Taylor glanced around, then opened a huge, black box inside the trunk. In several pieces lay the biggest gun Judd had ever seen. Beside it was a shell the size of a loaf of bread.

"No!" Judd said.

"As soon as he takes off, that chopper's falling from the sky."

Judd's mind reeled. He knew Rayford Steele was Nicolae's pilot. Was he flying the chopper? And if the potentate was assassinated, the Global Community would blame the witnesses. Judd couldn't let Taylor shoot it down.

Lionel was captivated by Carpathia and wondered whether he would try his mind-altering techniques. Buck Williams had described the potentate's ability to sway people, but

Lionel didn't know if it would work on a crowd filled mainly with believers.

"And so, my beloved friends," Carpathia said, "you do not have to join with the One World Faith to remain citizens of the Global Community. There is room for disagreement on matters of religion. But consider the advantages and benefits that have resulted from the uniting of every nation into one global village."

Nicolae gave a list of his achievements: everything from the repair of cities, roads, and airports to the rebuilding of New Babylon into the most magnificent city ever constructed. "It is a masterpiece I hope you will visit as soon as you can."

Lionel closed his eyes in thought. *One day Carpathia is going to declare himself god. With this kind of technology, Nicolae will be able to rule the world!*

As Lionel listened, he noticed something strange about Carpathia's voice. In the past, he had been always in command, never making a mistake, never struggling to remember a name or a date. Now he had grown hoarse. He turned away and cleared his throat. "Pardon me," he said, his voice still raspy. "I wish you and the rabbi here all the best and welcome you, . . . *ahem, ahem,* . . . excuse me—"

Nicolae turned to Tsion. "Would someone have some water?"

Dr. Ben-Judah didn't respond. Lionel saw someone in the front pass a bottle to the stage. Nicolae nodded and smiled. He unscrewed the cap, tipped it back for a long gulp, then gagged and spit it out. The crowd gasped. Nicolae's lips and chin were covered with blood. He held the bottle at arm's length, staring at it in fear.

Carpathia cursed at Tsion. "You and your evil flock of enemies! You would disgrace me like this for your own gain? I should have my men shoot you dead where you stand!"

Lionel saw two figures pass in the aisle near him. Both had long hair and wore tattered clothes. In unison Eli and Moishe spoke, without any microphone. The crowd fell back from around them, and the two stood in the eerie light of the stadium, shoulder to shoulder, barefoot.

"Woe unto you who would threaten the chosen vessel of the Most High God!"

Carpathia threw the bottle to the ground. Clear, clean water splashed everywhere.

Lionel looked around. Other people carried water bottles containing clear liquid. *Eli and Moishe caused his throat to parch,* Lionel thought. Nicolae pointed at the two and screamed, "Your time is nigh! I swear I will kill you or have you killed before—"

"Woe!" Eli and Moishe thundered, silencing Carpathia. "Woe to the impostor who would dare threaten the chosen ones before the due time! Sealed followers of the Messiah, drink deeply and be refreshed!"

A man beside Lionel took a long drink from a small bottle of water. He wiped his mouth and handed it to Lionel. "You drink now," he said.

The bottle was ice-cold and full. Lionel took a long drink. He handed it back to the man. Again, it was full. Throughout the stadium people sighed with pleasure at the taste. A few others tried to drink, but like Nicolae's bottle, the water turned to blood.

Lionel glanced at the stage. The chopper blades whirred to life, and Tsion was again alone. His notes flew around the stage like a tornado, then settled. People leaped to retrieve them. Tsion remained motionless, having ignored the entire episode with Carpathia.

Lionel looked around for the two witnesses, but they were gone.

Judd pleaded, but when the helicopter prepared for liftoff, Taylor picked up his weapon and placed it against his shoulder. The white chopper appeared over the top of the stadium and flew directly overhead.

Taylor aimed. Judd started to rush him, but before he did, Taylor dropped to the ground with the gun.

"It's them," Taylor gasped, his mouth hanging open.

Judd turned and saw Eli and Moishe walking toward them. They didn't say a word or even glance up as the helicopter passed. When they were gone, Taylor said, "I thought I was dead."

Judd helped him up. "You have to understand who you're dealing with. If you shot Carpathia down, the GC would blame the followers of Ben-Judah. They'd make us all martyrs tonight."

"I don't care. If that chopper returns, it's going down."

"Then I'll have to do what I have to do," Judd said, walking away.

"Which is what?" Taylor said.

The crowd around Lionel took their seats. Tsion was back at the lectern. As if nothing had happened since he began quoting John 3:16, Tsion continued:

"'—begotten Son, that whoever believes in Him should not perish but have everlasting life.'"

Tsion stepped back and repeated the verse louder as the helicopter flew away. "'For God so loved the world that He gave His only begotten Son, that whoever believes in Him should not perish but have everlasting life.'"

A man near Lionel fell to his knees. The man was holding a bottle filled with blood. Tsion said, "There may be some here, inside or outside, who want to receive Christ. I urge you to pray after me, 'Dear God, I know I am a sinner. Forgive me and pardon me for waiting so long. I receive your love and salvation and ask you to live your life through me. I accept you as my Savior and resolve to live for you until you come again.'"

As the man near Lionel repeated the prayer, the blood in the bottle changed to ice-cold water. The man stood. Lionel pointed at the bottle. The man raised it over his head, laughing, and let the liquid pour over him.

"I can see it," the man yelled, looking from one face to the next. "The cross on your foreheads. I see it!"

Others shouted, "Praise God!" and embraced one another.

Tsion stood at the lectern, his eyes brimming with tears, his hands clasped in front of his face in a posture of prayer.

Judd knew he had to tell someone about Taylor's plan. He pushed his way into the stadium and found a young guard with "Kudrick" on his name tag.

At first the guard told Judd to move along, but when Judd mentioned the high-powered weapon, the man radioed other guards and followed Judd outside. When they reached the area, Taylor was gone.

The guard pulled out a handheld computer and entered some data. Judd was sketchy about Taylor. "All I know is that this guy had a bazooka ready to fire at the potentate's helicopter, and the thing that stopped him was those two fire-breathing guys from the Wailing Wall."

The guard studied Judd. "Why are you here?"

"Curious," Judd said.

The guard put his computer away. "Do you know anything about the teaching of this Ben-Judah?"

"Are you asking for your report or because you're interested personally?"

The guard crossed his arms. "Does it matter?"

Suddenly an alarm went off on the guard's communication device. The guard plugged in his earphone, then pulled out his pistol and released the safety lock. He gave Judd a frantic look and ran back toward the stadium.

"Meet me right here tomorrow night," Judd yelled.

Judd wondered if he had just hurt the Young Trib Force by giving the GC information. Or had he made contact with a future follower of Christ?

Lionel waited for Judd. Though Dr. Ben-Judah had left the stage, people stood at the front, weeping, kneeling, and praying. As he watched, Lionel saw Mr. Stein walk across the stage and jump to the infield.

Lionel got Mr. Stein's attention, and the two embraced. Mr. Stein glowed with excitement. "I am overwhelmed. I had hoped you and Judd would be able to get inside."

"What happened to you?" Lionel said.

"You will not believe it. Yitzhak asked me to accompany him backstage as the group met for prayer before the message. I actually met Tsion Ben-Judah face-to-face."

"I bet he was surprised you were here in person."

"Very," Mr. Stein said. "I saw Buck and Chloe Williams backstage as well."

Nicolae Carpathia's helicopter appeared again. Judd rushed up and explained what had happened with Taylor Graham.

"You did the right thing," Mr. Stein said. "Taylor must be stopped."

"Something's wrong," Judd said. "The guard took off with his gun drawn."

"You don't think they're going to kill people, do you?" Lionel said.

Mr. Stein grabbed their arms. "Let's not give them the chance." The three raced for the nearest exit.

Above them, Leon Fortunato's voice boomed over the helicopter's loudspeakers. "We have been asked by Global Community ground security forces at the stadium to help clear this area! Please translate this message to others if at all possible! We appreciate your cooperation!"

Lionel ran ahead of Judd and Mr. Stein. The crowd did not obey. Hundreds of people moved to the corner of the stadium where the helicopter hovered.

As Lionel reached the stairs that would lead them outside, a machine gun fired outside the stadium. People screamed and dived for cover. Lionel kept moving, stepping over those on the ground. As the three made it outside, more shots filled the air.

TEN

Reason to Kill

VICKI switched the laptop to the sleep mode and sat back.

"I wonder how Carpathia's going to work this to his advantage." Conrad said. "I can't believe he lost his cool and cursed like that on live television."

"Can you imagine what the press will do with the water-to-blood thing?" Shelly said. "It's going to be plastered all over the headlines."

"Yeah, but the publicity will make everybody want to watch," Vicki said. "The meeting will be the biggest thing in TV history."

"If they let them continue," Conrad said.

Vicki sighed. An idea had been brewing since the beginning of Tsion's message. "I think we should change our clocks to Jerusalem time."

"What for?" Shelly said.

"The all-day meetings will begin just after midnight," Vicki said. "I know it's the middle of the afternoon, but if we get some sleep now, we can get up and watch the whole thing live."

The kids all agreed to try it. Vicki went to the kitchen to prepare what would be a midnight breakfast. Conrad said, "I want to see what Carpathia says about all this."

Vicki looked in on Melinda. Her door was slightly open. Vicki knocked and entered. "What did you think?"

Melinda shrugged. "Interesting. I've never seen the potentate that upset."

"What about the rabbi?" Vicki said.

"I guess he made some sense. A lot more than that Peter guy. But there's a lot I don't understand."

"Like what?"

"The stuff about the sheep," Melinda said.

"You mean the lamb?"

"Whatever."

Vicki sat on the bed. She explained that Jesus was the Lamb of God. "In the days before Jesus, God asked for a sacrifice for sins. I don't understand everything about it, but basically the people had to take a perfect lamb, kill it, then sprinkle its blood on an altar."

Melinda scowled. "That sounds weird. Why does God have to kill something? Can't he just look the other way?"

"The sacrifice reminded the people how bad sin is. Because God is holy, there has to be some kind of payment. That ceremony was sort of a picture of Jesus' sacrifice. He was the perfect Lamb who gave his life for us."

"I got it," Melinda said, "but I still think it's pretty weird."

Conrad knocked at the door. "You oughta come see this."

"We'll talk later," Vicki said.

The voice of Leon Fortunato echoed down the hall. "The supreme commander's introducing Nicolae," Conrad said.

"I don't believe this," Shelly groaned as Vicki came into the room. "This is the ultimate setup guy."

Fortunato looked calm and collected. He said there were still pockets of resistance to the progress of the Global Community. "One of those movements revealed its true nature earlier this evening before the eyes of the world."

"Yeah, they turned his drinking water to blood," Darrion said.

"His Excellency has the power to use

extreme measures because of this action, but in the spirit of the new society he has built, His Excellency has a different response he wishes to share with you.

"Before he does that, however, I would like to share a personal story."

"Uh-oh," Conrad said, "here it comes."

Fortunato told the world that after the earthquake, Nicolae Carpathia had raised him from the dead. He finished with, "And now, without further ado, your potentate and—may I say, my deity—His Excellency, Nicolae Carpathia."

"My deity?" Shelly said. "He thinks Carpathia's God?"

"Tsion said this would happen," Vicki said.

Fortunato bowed deeply and tried to make way for Carpathia, but he stumbled on a light cord and tumbled out of range of the camera. The kids laughed. Carpathia seemed flustered by the distraction, then quickly recovered.

"Fellow citizens, I am certain that if you did not see what happened earlier this evening at Teddy Kollek Stadium in Jerusalem, you have by now heard about it. Let me briefly tell you my view of what occurred and outline my response.

"One of my goals as a strong leader is tolerance. We can only truly be a global community by accepting our differences. It has been the clear wish of most of us that we break down walls and bring people together. Thus there is now one economy highlighted by one currency, no need for passports, one government, eventually one language, one system of measurement, and one religion."

Carpathia described Enigma Babylon One World Faith, which brought different religions under one banner. "Your way may be the only way for you, and my way the only way for me, but all religions of the world have proved themselves able to live in harmony."

Carpathia frowned. "All religions except one. You know the one. It is the sect that claims roots in historic Christianity. It holds that the vanishings of two and a half years ago were God's doing. Indeed, they say, Jesus blew a trumpet and took all his favorite people to heaven, leaving the rest of us lost sinners to suffer here on earth."

Carpathia crossed his arms and squinted. "This is not the truth of Christianity as it was taught for centuries. That wonderful, peace-loving religion told of a God of love and of a man who was a teacher of morals. His example was to be followed in order for a person to one day reach eternal heaven by continually improving oneself."

"This is too much," Vicki said. "If we reach heaven by improving ourselves, why did Jesus have to die?"

Carpathia continued. "Following the disappearances that caused such great chaos in our world, some misguided people looked to the Christian Bible for an explanation. They created a belief that said the true church was taken away."

"You think people are actually buying this?" Darrion said.

Carpathia referred to the followers of Dr. Ben-Judah as a cult. "I come to you tonight from the very studio where Dr. Ben-Judah turned his back on his own religion. While in exile, he has managed to brainwash thousands who are desperate. Dr. Ben-Judah has used the Internet for his own gain, no doubt taking millions from his followers. He has invented an us-against-them war."

"He hasn't taken a penny," Vicki shouted.

"For months I have ignored these harmless holdouts to world harmony. When Dr. Ben-Judah invited his converts to meet in the very city that had exiled him, I decided to allow it."

"Here comes the payoff," Conrad said. "He's about to bring the hammer down."

Carpathia held up his hands in a gesture of peace. "In a spirit of acceptance, I gave my public promise for Dr. Ben-Judah's safety. I believed the only right thing to do was to encourage this mass meeting. I wanted his followers to join us. But the choice was theirs. I would not have forced them.

"And how were my actions rewarded? Was I invited to the festivities? Allowed to bring a greeting or take part in any of the pageantry? No. I traveled to Israel at my own expense and dropped in to say a few words.

"My supreme commander was met with the rudeness of utter silence. The most revered Supreme Pontiff Peter the Second was received in the same manner, even though he is a fellow clergyman. This was obviously a well-planned mass response."

"A vast conspiracy," Conrad said.

"Shh," Vicki said. "Here's his explanation."

Carpathia accused Dr. Ben-Judah of controlling the minds of his audience. "I had the clear feeling that the crowd was with me. They wanted to welcome me. Dr. Ben-Judah somehow gave a signal to release an invisible dust or powder that instantly parched my throat and resulted in a powerful thirst.

"I should have been suspicious when I was immediately presented with a bottle from someone in the crowd. But as a trusting person, I assumed an unknown friend had come to my aid."

Carpathia gritted his teeth. "I was ambushed by a bottle of poisonous blood! It was such an obvious assassination attempt that I accused Dr. Ben-Judah right there. He had hidden in the crowd the two elderly lunatics from the Wailing Wall who have murdered several people. With hidden microphones turned louder than the one I was using, they shouted me down with threats.

"My doctor says if I had swallowed what they gave me, I would have died instantly."

Judd, Lionel, and Mr. Stein had fought their way through the crowd of frightened people to the safety of a nearby building. When the GC emergency vehicles left, the three headed for the gymnasium.

Judd was exhausted. He lay on his cot, listening to the prayers and conversation around him. Before he drifted off to sleep, Mr. Stein touched his shoulder and asked him to follow. "You'll want to see this."

A small group gathered around a television in an office near the front. Yitzhak sat with his feet on a desk. Judd recognized the man who had introduced Tsion onstage. His name was Daniel. Other members of the local committee stared at Nicolae Carpathia on TV.

Lionel brought Judd up to speed about Nicolae's speech. "He just said the assassination attempt is an act of high treason, punishable by death."

"Who are they going to execute, all of us?" Judd said.

Lionel shrugged.

Carpathia clenched his jaw. "There is no doubt that this ugly incident was engineered and carried out by Dr. Ben-Judah. But as a man of my word, I plan to allow the meetings to continue for the next two nights. I will maintain my pledge of security and protection."

"We do not need either from you," Daniel muttered.

Carpathia continued. "Dr. Ben-Judah, however, shall be exiled again from Israel within twenty-four hours of the end of the meeting. As for the two who call themselves Eli and Moishe, let this serve as public notification to them as well. For the next forty-eight hours, they shall be restricted to the area near the Wailing Wall. They are not to leave that area for any purpose at any time. When the meetings in the stadium have concluded, Eli and Moishe must leave the Temple Mount area. Their appearance anywhere but near the Wailing Wall for forty-eight hours or their showing their faces anywhere in the world after that shall be considered reason to kill. Any Global Community officer or private citizen is authorized to shoot to kill."

Yitzhak shook his head. "You will not kill the Lord's anointed until the due time."

"I know you will agree," Carpathia concluded, "that this is a most generous response to an ugly attack. Thank you, my friends, and good night from Israel."

As the news anchor recapped the story, Yitzhak turned off the television. "God is at work, my friends. Now we must rest. The next two days are very important."

Mr. Stein followed Judd and Lionel to their cots. "Before you sleep, you must know what has happened. There was an attempt on Tsion's life tonight."

"What?" Judd said.

"Somehow Tsion and the others found out that the guards were preparing to attack."

Judd gasped. "The guard I met was probably after Tsion! I'm hoping to meet him before tomorrow night's session."

Lionel scowled. "I don't know if we should get that close to a GC guard."

Judd asked how Tsion got away.

"He hid with Chloe in a utility room until

a friend created a diversion with gunfire,"
Mr. Stein said.

"So that's where the shots came from,"
Judd said. "Where are they now?"

"Tsion, Buck, and Chloe are staying at the
Chaim Rosenzweig estate." Mr. Stein leaned
close to the boys. "I am almost convinced I
am a true witness of God. I am going to see
Eli and Moishe now. I must talk to them."

Judd sighed. "I can hardly keep my eyes
open."

"I'll go," Lionel said.

Mr. Stein smiled. "I would be honored to
have you with me." He looked at Judd. "I
may not be able to spend much time with
you over the next two days. Drink in as much
of the teaching as you can."

Mr. Stein led them in a prayer. Judd fell
back on his cot and was asleep in minutes.

ELEVEN

The Consuming Fire

LIONEL rode with Mr. Stein in Yitzhak's car. They took a wrong turn and drove through a shabby part of Jerusalem. Drunks staggered about the streets. Bars, fortune-telling shops, tattoo parlors, and strip clubs advertised in glaring lights.

"Yitzhak told me about this," Mr. Stein said, turning the car around. "The new religion welcomes any belief system. Hedonism is rampant."

"Hedonism?" Lionel said.

"Pleasures of the flesh. Whatever feels good. This is what happens when people buy into the lie that God is whoever we want him to be."

Mr. Stein found the right road and made it to the Wailing Wall. When they arrived, a GC guard was making an announcement.

"Attention, ladies and gentlemen! I have been asked by the Global Community supreme commander to remind citizens of the proclamation from His Excellency, Potentate Nicolae Carpathia, that the two men you see before you are under house arrest. They are confined to this area until the end of the Meeting of the Witnesses Friday night. If they leave this area before that, any GC personnel or private citizen is within his rights to detain them by force, to wound them, or to kill them. Further, if they are seen anywhere, repeat, *anywhere*, following that time, they shall be put to death."

A huge crowd near the fence cheered wildly, laughed, and jeered at the witnesses. Eli and Moishe seemed not to notice the guard or those nearby who spat at them.

Gigantic lights lit the area. The witnesses were bathed in a glaring spotlight, but they didn't squint or blink.

"So much for a quiet conversation," Lionel said. "Since Carpathia's new law, the media's crawling everywhere."

Mr. Stein took Lionel to the bushes where they had been before. The crowd cheered when a man suggested he wanted to kill the witnesses.

Barely moving his lips, Eli spoke at the top of his lungs. At the force of his voice, the crowd stumbled back. "Come nigh and question not this warning from the Lord of Hosts. He who would dare come against the appointed servants of the Most High God, the same shall surely die!"

When the crowd inched forward, taunting again, Eli erupted a second time. "Tempt not the chosen ones, for if you come against the voices crying in the wilderness, God himself will consume your flesh!"

A man held up a high-powered rifle and laughed. The GC guards spoke to the man, but Lionel couldn't hear them. Mr. Stein tugged on Lionel's arm. "They're moving!"

Eli and Moishe disappeared behind the slope. Mr. Stein stood. "If we can make it to the other side of the hill, I may be able to speak to them."

Lionel ran through the dewy grass, following Mr. Stein to the bottom of the hill. Behind them the GC guard spoke urgently. "Search the area behind the fence! If the two are not there, they are in violation of the potentate and may be shot!"

"The Mount of Olives!" Mr. Stein whispered.

Lionel gasped for air as they climbed. Finally they spotted the two at the top of a knoll beside a lone olive tree. Mr. Stein bent double, his hands on his knees. They were ten feet from the two witnesses.

"Please," Mr. Stein gasped. "I am a Jew. I believe Jesus is the Messiah. Can I know if I am truly a witness of the Most High God?"

Moishe didn't speak but motioned for them to get behind a tree. Crowds ran up the hill, shouting murderous threats.

Eli and Moishe spoke at the same time. They looked directly at Mr. Stein and said, "Harken unto us, servants of the Lord God Almighty, Maker of heaven and earth!"

The witnesses were suddenly bathed in light, not from the news cameras or anything earthly, but from a heavenly glow. The sight was awesome.

Eli and Moishe warned the mob that they would be devoured by fire if they tried to hurt God's servants. "We have been granted the power to shut heaven, that it rain not in the days of our prophecy. Yea, we have power over waters to turn them to blood and to smite the earth with all plagues, as often as we will.

"And what is our prophecy? That Jesus of Bethlehem, the son of the Virgin Mary, was in the beginning with God, and he was God, and he is God. Yea, he fulfilled all the prophecies of the coming Messiah, and he shall reign and rule now and forevermore, world without end, amen!"

Lionel looked down the hill. The people ignored the warnings. "I don't like the looks of this."

"It is ours to bring rain," the witnesses shouted. A freezing gush of water poured from the skies and drenched the ground.

"Yitzhak said it has not rained here in twenty-four months!" Mr. Stein said, shivering.

The rain stopped a moment later.

"And it is ours to shut heaven for the days of our prophecy!" the witnesses proclaimed.

Lionel heard the murmurs and threats of the crowd. They were a hundred yards away and tramping through the mud.

"You got your answer when they called you a servant of God," Lionel said. "We should get out of here."

Before Mr. Stein could move, the prophets stopped the crowd with their booming voices. Eli and Moishe spoke against the new temple. They called it blasphemy. "Your sacrifices of animal blood are a stench in the nostrils of your God! Turn from your wicked ways, O sinners! Advance not against the chosen ones whose time has not yet been accomplished!"

Lionel peeked from behind the tree. Two GC guards rushed up the hill, weapons raised. They slipped on the wet hillside and fell to the ground.

"Woe unto you who would close your ears to the warnings of the chosen ones!" the witnesses shouted. "Flee to the caves to save yourselves! Your mission is doomed! Your bodies shall be consumed!"

The guards crawled on their bellies. The crowd shouted to the guards, "Kill them! Shoot them!"

Gunfire exploded. Lionel heard a *ping* and looked up. A bullet left a gash in the tree just above his head. The witnesses remained steady, unmoving, unhurt. They stood, still illuminated on the hill. The guards reloaded and fired again. Lionel and Mr. Stein huddled together.

A flash of light and a *whooshing* sound surrounded them. The air was filled with an intense heat. The gunshots were replaced with a sizzling fire. Lionel looked down the hill and saw the two guards engulfed in flames. They had no time to react. Within seconds the white heat turned their rifles to puddles of boiling liquid and their bones to ash. The crowd fled, screaming, cursing, and crying.

"Let's go," Mr. Stein said.

Lionel looked back only once more. The witnesses were walking slowly down the hill toward the Wailing Wall.

Vicki awoke at 11 P.M. Midwest time. It was pitch-black outside, and there wasn't a sound in the rest of the house. She went to the meeting room and searched the Web to find coverage of the all-day training. It would begin at midnight her time.

The numbers reported by the media were staggering. Twenty-five thousand had been in Teddy Kollek Stadium the night before. More than fifty thousand had gathered outside. Another report said the two preachers at the Wailing Wall had violated the potentate's directive. Two guards had been murdered trying to apprehend them. Eyewitnesses on the Mount of Olives accused the two of hiding flamethrowers in their robes. The weapons had not been recovered, and the preachers were reported back in their usual spots.

Vicki scoffed at the report and wondered what the real story was. She opened her Bible and went through the passages Tsion had read during the first meeting. She wrote out a prayer in her notebook. "God, show us what you want us to do. I put myself and all of the Young Trib Force in your hands. Amen."

Listening to the meeting the day before had given Vicki an idea. The evening sessions seemed mainly for encouragement, motivation, and Tsion's teaching. She could only imagine the feeling of worshiping God with thousands of other believers, hearing the words of their earthly leader firsthand. But the bulk of the training to evangelize the world would occur during the all-day sessions. Vicki and the others could memorize that teaching and train other kids.

She quickly sketched out a plan of action. They would record the sessions onto the computer's hard drive, just as they were recording Tsion's messages. The kids would then write out the lessons in a way anyone could understand.

At 11:30, Vicki set out the food and awakened the others. Conrad nodded when he heard Vicki's plan. "This could help us answer some of the E-mail Tsion is getting from kids."

Judd awoke, refreshed, and found his way to the morning session. Lionel was still asleep. The meetings were open on a first-come, first-served basis. When one location filled, participants moved to the next site. The teacher at Judd's seminar was Yitzhak. Judd was amazed that such a humble man was actually one of the leaders.

After a song and prayer, Yitzhak tackled the subject of speaking one-on-one with unbelievers. "Though many of us have come to faith via the Internet or watching the mass media, we must not underestimate the importance of talking with individuals."

Yitzhak outlined a series of questions. "Do not use these as a list to check off. If you are not interested in the other person, he or she will know it and will sense you are asking in a selfish way. If you can, get to know the other person. Many have gone through tragic circumstances. They have lost loved ones. They are separated from family members. Remember that the Good News must be accompanied by true compassion."

Judd believed each member of the Young Trib Force had already followed these principles. Their work on the *Underground* and Judd's message at graduation proved how much they were willing to risk. Now Judd felt like being even bolder with people one-on-one.

"We only have a limited time," Yitzhak said. "If someone does not respond to the message, pray for that person. Then ask God to lead you to someone else who needs the hope of eternal life."

Speaker after speaker circulated through

the meeting places. By the end of the day,
Judd had taken in an incredible amount of
information.

He met with Lionel for dinner at the gymnasium and found out what had happened
with Eli and Moishe the night before.
"Because of the death of the two guards,"
Lionel said, "security is supposed to be really
tight tonight."

"I almost forgot," Judd said, looking at his
watch. "I was supposed to meet the guard!"

Vicki and the others took turns taking notes
during the early morning sessions. When she
heard one man talk about speaking to people
one-on-one, she thought of Melinda and
Charlie. Melinda stayed away from the day-
time sessions, but Charlie watched. He began
to ask questions, and Vicki had to take him
out of the room.

Charlie seemed upset. "I don't have that
thing on my head," he said. Vicki questioned
him once more about what he thought had
happened during the disappearances.

"That's easy," Charlie said. "All the good
people got taken up to heaven, and the bad
people stayed down here."

She explained that afternoon and again at

dinner that those who were raptured weren't better than those left behind—they had just been forgiven. "How much good stuff do you have to do to get into heaven?" Vicki said.

"Enough so that the good stuff is more than the bad?" Charlie said.

"No," Vicki said. "Even if you do only one bad thing, God has to reject you because he's holy."

Charlie nodded, but Vicki knew he still didn't get it.

Conrad rushed into the room. "You have to see this."

Vicki rushed to the meeting room and saw an urgent E-mail on the screen. "Is it from Judd?"

Conrad shook his head. "This is really weird."

Vicki scanned the message. It simply said, *Need to talk to Mark immediately. Let me know how I can find him. A friend.*

"Who could it be from?" Vicki said.

"Look at the return address," Conrad said.

Vicki gasped. It was from a GC military post.

As thousands streamed toward the stadium, Judd and Lionel looked for the guard. GC guards looked threateningly at the growing crowds. Judd could tell by the conversation of those around him that many were skeptics, curious about the meeting.

"Let's separate," Judd said as the meeting time approached. "He might think I'm up to something if he sees somebody with me."

"It's your funeral," Lionel said, walking away.

A few minutes later the guard approached Judd, his rifle ready.

"I'm glad you came," Judd said. "I wanted to talk to you about—"

The guard interrupted. "You heard about the two who were killed last night?"

Judd nodded.

"I was supposed to be on duty there," the guard said. "My friend took my place and now he's dead."

Judd thought of the guards who had been burned alive.

"You and your kind are the reason he's dead."

"You've had a terrible loss," Judd said, "but don't blame us. God loves you and wants to get your attention."

The guard pushed Judd away. "If I get the okay, the people onstage are dead."

TWELVE

Death in the Stadium

Vicki and the others tried to figure out who had written the E-mail and what they should do. As difficult as it was to put it out of their minds, they decided to leave the E-mail unanswered until after the Meeting of the Witnesses was over.

After the early sessions were complete, the kids ate. Some slept, while others went outside to walk or get some fresh air. Conrad had found an old baseball and a tree limb about the size of a bat. He tried to get others to join him, but no one seemed interested.

The meeting began at 11 A.M. with cheers and applause for Tsion. He smiled and raised his hands for silence.

"You have learned much today," Tsion began, "and I have warned you of many judgments. I will tell you now what to expect next.

When it occurs, let no man deny that he was warned and that this warning has been recorded in the Scriptures for centuries."

Tsion explained that God doesn't want anyone to die without being forgiven of their sin. "That is the reason for this entire season of trial. In his love and mercy God has tried everything to get our attention. Is there doubt in anyone's mind that all of this is God's doing?

"Repent! Turn to him. Accept his gift before it is too late. It is likely that three-fourths of everyone left behind at the Rapture will die by the end of the Tribulation.

"I want to tell you tonight of the fourth Trumpet Judgment that will affect the look of the skies and the temperature of the entire globe. Revelation 8:12 reads, 'Then the fourth angel sounded: And a third of the sun was struck, a third of the moon, and a third of the stars, so that a third of them were darkened. A third of the day did not shine, and likewise the night.'"

Tsion explained that this judgment would cause great distress on the earth. "Prophecy indicates this darkening and cooling is temporary. But when it occurs it will usher in—for however long—winterlike conditions in most of the world. Prepare, prepare, prepare!"

"It's a good thing we have a generator that works," Conrad said. "We'd freeze out here."

"The glorious appearing of Jesus Christ is fewer than five years away," Tsion said. "I believe the greatest time of harvest is now, before the second half of the Tribulation, which the Bible calls the Great Tribulation.

"One day the evil world system will require the bearing of a mark in order for its citizens to buy or sell. You may rest assured it will not be the mark we see on each other's foreheads!

"You must begin to store food and other provisions for what is to come. Above all, we must trust God. He expects us to be wise as serpents and gentle as doves.

"Tomorrow night I'm afraid I have a difficult message to bring. You may get a preview of it by reading Revelation 9."

It was afternoon in Illinois, but the kids were exhausted. Vicki and the others went to their rooms. She couldn't get the E-mail out of her mind. Had the GC found them? Was Mark in some kind of trouble?

Before she went to sleep, Vicki opened her Bible. Her hands trembled as she read.

Judd awoke early Friday and spent the day in a blur of activity. The all-day meetings focused on the importance of the message and gave specific texts of Scripture to memorize. "These are the words of God," one speaker said, "and God's words are effective. Use them well."

Late in the afternoon, Judd and Lionel walked to the stadium early to make sure they got seats. At the east entrance they were amazed to see the crowds already standing shoulder to shoulder. Most were Jewish believers, but many were also skeptics and seekers who had seen the coverage and wanted to view Dr. Ben-Judah themselves.

"Can you believe Carpathia's news media has covered this whole thing?" Lionel said.

"Probably Nick's way of keeping track of everything they say," Judd said.

Again, Judd looked for the GC guard but couldn't find him. He and Lionel made their way into the already packed stadium. As darkness fell, Judd spotted the guard near the stage. "Save my seat. I'll be right back."

"I can't talk to you," the guard said as Judd approached, his eyes darting toward the stage.

Judd turned his back and kept talking. "Why not?"

"Get out of here—"

"Just answer this," Judd said. "You've listened the last two nights. Does Tsion's message make sense?"

"I'm telling you, I can't talk," the guard said.

"Tell me, is any of it getting through?"

The guard looked down and whispered, "Last night I listened and wondered what would have happened . . . if those two preachers had zapped me instead of my friend."

Judd felt a ray of hope for the guard.

"At first, I thought you people were crazy, all the praying and singing. Last night I was ready to kill everyone on the stage. Now, I don't know. I wonder if I've done something wrong."

"We all have," Judd said. "That's the point. But God's trying to get our attention. Let me tell you what we believe. I can help."

The guard stole a glance around the stage. "You have to go. The other guards will see us."

"If you ask God to forgive you, he will," Judd said. "You can become one of us."

"How would you know I wasn't a GC spy?"

Judd smiled. "Trust me, I'll know." Judd quickly explained what it meant to be a believer. The guard listened. Suddenly the man's radio squawked.

"I have to go," the guard said, "but I want to talk again afterward. Meet me here by the stage when everyone is gone."

Judd walked away. He prayed Tsion would say something to get through to the guard.

Judd made it back to his seat as Daniel announced a rally at the Temple Mount the following day. "What's that about?" Judd said.

"A thank-you to the local committee," Lionel said. "We ought to go."

A few moments later Daniel said, "And now I invite you to listen to a message from the Word of God."

As Tsion Ben-Judah walked to the podium, the crowd rose and clapped. There was no shouting, cheering, or whistling. The response overwhelmed Tsion. He put his notes on the lectern and waited for the applause to end.

"God has put something on my heart tonight," Tsion said. "Even before I open his Word, I feel led to invite seekers to come forward and receive Christ."

Immediately, from all over the stadium and even outside, lines of people, many weeping, began streaming forward, causing another burst of applause. Judd couldn't believe how many were coming. He wondered if those watching over the Global Community's outlets were praying as well.

Tsion said, "You do not have to be with us physically to receive Christ tonight. All you need to do is to tell God you are a sinner and separated from him. Tell him you know that nothing you can do will earn your way to him. Tell him you believe that he sent his Son, Jesus Christ, to die on the cross for your sins, that Jesus was raised from the dead, and that he is coming again to the earth. Receive him as your Savior right where you are."

After nearly an hour, the people who had come forward headed back to their seats. Tsion looked tired. His shoulders sagged. When he spoke, his voice was weak.

"My text tonight is Revelation 8:13." Tens of thousands of Bibles opened around the stadium. "This passage warns that once the earth has been darkened by one-third, three terrible woes will follow. These are so horrible that they will be announced from heaven in advance."

Lionel grabbed Judd's arm. "Look!"

Emerging from the shadows of the stage behind Tsion were Eli and Moishe. They walked to the front as the crowd pointed and leaned forward to hear them.

Moishe said, "My beloved brethren, the God of all grace, who hath called us unto his eternal glory by Christ Jesus, after that ye have suffered a while, make you perfect, stablish, strengthen, settle you."

Then Moishe loudly quoted Tsion's passage for everyone to hear. "'And I beheld, and heard an angel flying through the midst of heaven, saying with a loud voice, "Woe, woe, woe, to the inhabiters of the earth by reason of the other voices of the trumpet of the three angels, which are yet to sound!"'"

GC guards engaged their rifles, but no one fired. Judd wanted to run to the guard he knew and hold him back. Judd closed his eyes, ready for the gunfire, but when he opened them he saw Eli and Moishe were gone. Guards scrambled everywhere.

Tsion shook. Whether from fear or excitement, Judd couldn't say. To Judd's surprise, Tsion said, "If we never meet again this side of heaven or in the millennial kingdom our Savior sets up on earth, I shall greet you on the Internet and teach from Revelation 9! Godspeed as you share the gospel of Christ with the whole world!"

The Meeting of the Witnesses was over. Tsion disappeared into the shadows. Judd leaped to his feet, while the aisle was clear, and ran toward the front.

"They're ending early," Vicki said as the kids watched the wrap-up of the final session.

Conrad was deep in thought. "If Tsion's right, we're going to spend the rest of our lives as criminals. We won't be able to trust anyone."

"With the GC in control of everything," Shelly said, "we'll have to scramble just to stay alive."

Vicki heard a noise. Scratching. She opened the front door but didn't see anything. The noise was coming from the back of the house. She rushed into the kitchen. The noise got louder. She checked the back door.

Nothing.

Then Vicki realized the noise was coming from Melinda's room.

Before Judd could get past, the crowd filed into the aisles. He pushed his way around the last person and rushed toward the front.

"Let's figure out a place to meet," Judd said as he made it to the guard. The man turned. It was a different guard. "Sorry," Judd said.

Judd moved along the front of the stage. People craned their necks to get a glimpse of Tsion. Others knelt and wept.

Judd finally located the guard, but he could tell something was different. The guard held his gun high, his helmet pulled low. When he saw Judd he put a finger to his lips.

He touched his earpiece and said something into the microphone on his shoulder.

"You have to leave," the guard said.

"I'm not going until I talk with you," Judd said.

"You don't understand," the guard said. "People are going to be killed here tonight. Leave!"

"What people?" Judd said. "Who?"

The guard lowered his voice. "My job is to keep everyone away from the backstage area. You're not safe here. Meet me at the east entrance in an hour."

"Tell me—"

The guard pushed his helmet up so Judd could see his forehead. Judd gasped as he saw the mark of the true believer.

"Go now," the guard said.

Judd rushed back to Lionel and told him about the guard. "I have to hear his story!" Lionel said. They looked for Mr. Stein but couldn't find him. Slowly they filed out behind the thousands who would take the message of the gospel to the ends of the earth.

As they reached the top of the stairs, Judd looked down on the infield. The guard was talking to someone. Suddenly, the man bolted onto the stage. The guard yelled, "Wait! Stop! Assistance!"

"That's Buck Williams!" Lionel shouted.

The guard aimed his rifle and fired.

"He's going to kill him!" Lionel shouted.

At the sound of the gunfire, frightened people pushed toward the exit. Some fell in the panic. Others tried to help them but were pushed along with the crowd.

"I've got to get down there," Judd yelled.

Vicki opened Melinda's door. Phoenix whimpered on the floor, his legs taped together. Around his snout was another wide band of tape.

"How long have you been here, boy?" Vicki said as she struggled to free the dog.

Vicki looked out the window. She had been so engrossed in the teaching of Dr. Ben-Judah that she had forgotten about Melinda.

Vicki shook her head. "Where's she going?"

Judd led Lionel toward the infield, walking on the backs of seats. Several times Judd nearly lost his balance, but they finally made it to the infield and sprinted toward the guard. The man's gun was still smoking. Judd shouted. The guard turned, saw Judd, and waved his hands. "Get down!" the guard yelled.

Judd and Lionel hit the ground just as another round of gunfire erupted. People screamed as the *pop pop pop* of shots rang out near the stage.

On his knees, Judd looked for the guard. The man lay in a pool of blood. Three bullet holes had pierced his chest. Judd lifted the man's head.

The guard gasped for air. "I prayed tonight. I asked God to forgive me. Thank you for helping me see the truth."

"Why did you shoot at that man?" Judd said. "He's one of us!"

"I know," the guard choked. "We had orders to shoot the rabbi. I shot over Mr. Williams's head to distract the other guards. They must have figured it out and turned their guns on me."

The guard closed his eyes. "What happens to me now? Where will I—"

"You'll see God," Judd said. "When you wake up, you'll be in heaven."

The guard smiled. He grabbed Judd's arm. "Get out while you can."

Judd felt for a pulse. The guard was dead. Above them came the pounding of footsteps. The other guards were on the stage searching for Tsion Ben-Judah.

ABOUT THE AUTHORS

Jerry B. Jenkins (www.jerryjenkins.com) is the writer of the Left Behind series. He is author of more than one hundred books, of which eleven have reached the *New York Times* best-seller list. Former vice president for publishing for the Moody Bible Institute of Chicago, he also served many years as editor of *Moody* magazine and is now Moody's writer-at-large.

His writing has appeared in publications as varied as *Reader's Digest*, *Parade*, in-flight magazines, and many Christian periodicals. He has written books in four genres: biography, marriage and family, fiction for children, and fiction for adults.

Jenkins's biographies include books with Hank Aaron, Bill Gaither, Luis Palau, Walter Payton, Orel Hershiser, Nolan Ryan, Brett Butler, and Billy Graham, among many others.

Eight of his apocalyptic novels—*Left Behind, Tribulation Force, Nicolae, Soul Harvest, Apollyon, Assassins, The Indwelling,* and *The Mark*—have appeared on the Christian Booksellers Association's best-selling fiction list and the *Publishers Weekly* religion best-seller list. *Left Behind* was nominated for Book of the Year by the Evangelical Christian Publishers Association in 1997, 1998, 1999, and 2000. *The Indwelling* was number one on the *New York Times* best-seller list for four consecutive weeks.

As a marriage and family author and speaker, Jenkins has been a frequent guest on Dr. James Dobson's *Focus on the Family* radio program.

Jerry is also the writer of the nationally syndicated sports story comic strip *Gil Thorp,* distributed to newspapers across the United States by Tribune Media Services.

Jerry and his wife, Dianna, live in Colorado.

Dr. Tim LaHaye (www.timlahaye.com), who conceived the idea of fictionalizing an account of the Rapture and the Tribulation, is a noted author, minister, and nationally recognized speaker on Bible prophecy. He is the founder of both Tim LaHaye Ministries and The Pre-Trib Research Center. Presently Dr. LaHaye speaks at many of the major Bible prophecy conferences in the U.S. and Canada, where his nine current prophecy books are very popular.

Dr. LaHaye holds a doctor of ministry degree from Western Theological Seminary and the doctor of literature degree from Liberty University. For twenty-five years he pastored one of the nation's outstanding churches in San Diego, which grew to three locations. It was during that time that he founded two accredited Christian high schools, a Christian school system of ten schools, and Christian Heritage College.

Dr. LaHaye has written over forty books, with over 30 million copies in print in thirty-three languages. He has written books on a wide variety of subjects, such as family life, temperaments, and Bible prophecy. His current fiction works, written with Jerry Jenkins—*Left Behind, Tribulation Force, Nicolae, Soul Harvest, Apollyon, Assassins, The Indwelling,* and *The Mark*—have all reached number one on the Christian best-seller charts. Other works by Dr. LaHaye are *Spirit-Controlled Temperament; How to Be Happy Though Married; Revelation Unveiled; Understanding the Last Days; Rapture under Attack; Are We Living in the End Times?;* and the youth fiction series Left Behind: The Kids.

He is the father of four grown children and grandfather of nine. Snow skiing, waterskiing, motorcycling, golfing, vacationing with family, and jogging are among his leisure activities.

The Future Is Clear

Check out the exciting Left Behind: The Kids series

#1: The Vanishings

#2: Second Chance

#3: Through the Flames

#4: Facing the Future

#5: Nicolae High

#6: The Underground

#7: Busted!

#8: Death Strike

#9: The Search

#10: On the Run

#11: Into the Storm

#12: Earthquake!

#13: The Showdown

#14: Judgment Day

#15: Battling the Commander

#16: Fire from Heaven

#17: Terror in the Stadium

#18: Darkening Skies

BOOKS #19 AND #20 COMING SOON!

Discover the latest about the Left Behind series and complete line of products at

www.leftbehind.com